Lisa,

Every child is a Miracle
wrapped in the image of God.

MJ Hutchinson

WASHINGTON PARK

A Novel

Michael Irvin Hutchinson, MD

Inspiring Voices®
A Service of **Guideposts**

Inspiring Voices books may be ordered through booksellers or by contacting:

Inspiring Voices
1663 Liberty Drive
Bloomington, IN 47403
www.inspiringvoices.com
1-(866) 697-5313

Because of the dynamic nature of the Internet, any web addresses or links contained in this book may have changed since publication and may no longer be valid. The views expressed in this work are solely those of the author and do not necessarily reflect the views of the publisher, and the publisher hereby disclaims any responsibility for them.

Any people depicted in stock imagery provided by Shutterstock are models, and such images are being used for illustrative purposes only.

Certain stock imagery © Shutterstock.

ISBN: 978-1-4624-0231-1 (sc)
ISBN: 978-1-4624-0232-8 (hc)
ISBN: 978-1-4624-0230-4 (e)

Library of Congress Control Number: 2012943673

Printed in the United States of America

Inspiring Voices rev. date: 08/01/2012

Illustrations

Pat, the boys' Boston terrier 7
Elfindale Lake, Springfield, Missouri 14
Maple Park Cemetery 19
Greene County Courthouse 35
Stone Chapel, Drury College campus 45
City Hall and Post Office 75
Blue, the best bloodhound on Earth 118
Gilbert's Gas Station 164
Michael and Blue 169

For my loving wife, Glenda

Preface

When was the last time something extraordinary happened to you, something you could not explain? There are many documented events throughout human history that defy explanation. These events, which baffle our common sense and intelligence, seem to live only in our imagination. But people do accomplish miraculous things. For example, a man lifts a two-thousand-pound car off a victim trapped underneath or rescues a person from the rubble of a building four days after a tornado. You may have heard about comatose patients in the hospital who suddenly awaken after many months or years of silence with normal brain function. Are these events always due to chance alone?

The scientists tell us the big bang occurred fourteen billion years ago and set in motion an evolutionary process that one day produced that which we see all around us on this tiny, unique planet called Earth. They say that's just the way the universe works and all that we can see is the inevitable outcome of the fusion of hydrogen atoms by distant stars. It all happened by chance through a process of combining atoms into molecules. The binding together of these molecules eventually formed living tissue. This primitive tissue developed into living, breathing, and thinking carbon-based life forms through billions of years of evolution. Thus far, this evolutionary process has brought us mankind, the reality we live in now.

But we know so little about ourselves. How can we know what lies beyond? What if there was a plan for this reality we see around us? What if the same thing that is happening here is happening on other planets? What if similar civilizations have lived and died in the distant past of eternity? How will we ever know? There exist thirty billion trillion stars in our universe alone. How do we know for sure if our universe is the only one in the vastness of infinite space? What is the likelihood that many advanced civilizations exist today throughout our own universe? The "chances" are very good that the same chemical and biological processes that produced our reality are occurring elsewhere. If so, do they have the same emotions we have, such as love, anger, happiness, regret, loneliness, resentment, greed, hope, or charity?

Our feelings about the purpose of life come from our belief that life must have some meaning. Not everything happens by chance alone, or does it? A mother is taking her children to school. She is delayed briefly as she speaks to her neighbor before pulling out of her driveway. As she drives her car down the street, she sees a terrible accident ahead. If she had not been delayed by her neighbor, it would have resulted in their deaths. Did that happen by chance alone? Are the events in our lives all related to each other even though they seem totally unrelated? Do we follow one path in our life from birth to death, or do we take many new, different, and unrelated paths every day? Do we truly have free will?

No one knows the answers to these questions. But we do know that everyone goes to bed each night hoping tomorrow will be a better day than today. Everyone feels the emotions of love, hope, sacrifice, sharing, happiness, sadness, anger, peace, and loss. If we on Earth are unique in these emotions, why were we given these emotions, and other civilizations were not? And finally, if we are unique, who made us so? Our time here is very brief, just a single note in the endless symphony of the universe. When you contemplate how truly insignificant our planet is in size, time, and space, it is hard to imagine that we could exist at all. But we do exist, and each of our lives has meaning.

Regardless of your situation in this life, all people have within themselves a faith that gives them encouragement day after day. Faith comes from many sources, most of which are within our control or in control of those around us. When you have faith in the idea that you or your loved ones can help you to have a better day tomorrow, then you have hope. If you have hope, you have life. Without faith or hope, you have nothingness, and what happens tomorrow doesn't really matter.

However, it matters a great deal to those with hope in the benevolent Creator who placed us here. This simple act of faith will give you hope that we exist for some future and worthwhile purpose. We all will choose, in our own way, whether we believe there is more to our lives than this life alone or that when this life is over, it's over. I choose to believe that both the energy and soul of our lives are eternal.

This is a story about hope. It took place forty years ago in a small Southwest Missouri town of Springfield. It illustrates some of the deep emotions people experience unexpectedly in their otherwise routine lives. Most importantly, it shows us that when all seems lost, we are saved by that unseen force of redemption.

Or maybe it was just by chance.

My hope is that you enjoy the story. I welcome your comments about the book and about the amazing and unexplainable events that may have happened in your life. Please send them to me at mihutchinsonmd@aol.com.

You can't live a perfect day without doing something for someone who will never be able to repay you.
—*John Wooden, Coach of the UCLA Bruins, 1948–75*

Chapter One

The bright sunlight reflected off the heavy snow piled high on the front lawn and pierced the windows of the bedroom. It caught the sleepy eyes of the two brothers, forcing them to bury their heads deep into their pillows. The entire neighborhood was just waking up after yesterday's Christmas 1959 celebrations. The Christmas routine at the Porter home was pretty much the same from year to year. The presents were opened early, followed by the Christmas sermon at church and the customary visit to Grandma Kate's house for dinner in Ozark, Missouri, just south of Springfield. Grandma always cooked one of her two specialties, fried chicken or chicken with dumplings.

The two boys loved their grandma Kate, who'd had an active part in their upbringing ever since her husband passed away four years before. The family had a very interesting history, handed down from their ancestors in the eleventh century in England. Grandpa Edward's family records indicated that his distant grandfather on his mother's side fought for control of England during that period. Following the overthrow of the king, the Cornett family worked in the royal court before returning to farming as their sole source of subsistence. In the year 1871, the family left England and settled in Grayson County, Virginia. Grandpa Ed's mother was Margaret Elliott Cornett, granddaughter of William Cornett Sr., who brought the family to Virginia from England. Margaret married William

Porter, whose family had been landowners and farmers. When Edward was a small boy, William Porter moved his family from their southwestern Virginia farm on November 30, 1881, and arrived in Southwest Missouri on January 4, 1882. No one knows why they decided to make the trip during the winter.

Edward married Kate, a local girl from Ozark, in 1910, and they had six children. They lived on a four-hundred-acre farm just north of town and continued the family tradition of living off the land. It was true that the Porter family's ancestors had been fighting the English kings seven hundred years before Washington did, and they seemed proud of that fact.

It was always fun to visit Grandma Kate for Sunday dinner, which the boys did every other week. The day was full of laughter, playing in the snow, and great food. But best of all, in addition to the deep snow covering Southwest Missouri, school was out for another week. A whole week filled with snow and no school. What could be better than that!

Stephen Lowell Porter and his brother, Michael David Porter, had waited for this day ever since last winter. Today was the day for the big game. The boys, nicknamed Spud and Spike, had waited all year for the deep cold of winter and the brief season for hockey. The last ten days had seen very cold weather in the Ozarks, and the lakes were frozen in perfect condition. The boys were born in the year of 1945, just ten months apart. Spud was given his name because he was a little heavier than his brother and always wanted a potato at every meal. He sure did love potatoes! No one really knew how Spike got his name. It just had always been so.

They were now fourteen years old and inseparable. They did everything together. They even stayed home from school if the other one was sick. They were in the same class at school and the same Sunday school class at church, and they joined the same sports teams. Everyone thought they were twins. On this day, they would lead their team to victory on the ice. It took no more than two minutes to get dressed and to arrive at the kitchen table for breakfast.

Also, arising from the floor between the boys' beds was Pat. He was the boys' ever-present companion. Pat was a large, sixty-pound Boston terrier that accompanied them everywhere. He waited by the back door for them to return from school and, when they were home, never left their side. He was their friend, playmate, protector, and confidant. Once after school, the neighborhood bully was pushing Spud around, trying to pick a fight. Pat jumped on him and pinned him to the ground. He then let Spud beat the tar out of him before letting him go. They didn't see much of that kid anymore, and, of course, Mom never found out.

Mom and Dad were products of the Depression Era and brought the boys up in a fairly strict, conservative household. They didn't have a lot of luxuries, but they had what they needed. They also had a lot of love between them. Mom knew the boys had a big day planned, and she was up early cooking breakfast. The kitchen was filled with the aroma of hot syrup and pancakes with chocolate milk and a potato for Spud.

Springfield is a small town in the southwestern part of the state, and not much occurred there of national importance. The town is near the geographical center of the country and is a combination of both city and rural life. Like most midwestern cities, Springfield began as a ranching and farming community. It is the birthplace of Route 66, which connected the Great Lakes to the Pacific Ocean. It is situated on the Ozark Plateau, in the center of the Ozark Mountains. These mountains stretch from Fayetteville, Arkansas, north almost to Jefferson City, Missouri.

Nicknamed the Queen City of the Ozarks, Springfield is proud of its heritage. Missouri developed from the westward expansion following the purchase of the Louisiana Territory from Spain by President Thomas Jefferson in 1803. Missouri became a state in 1821 and was named after the Missouri Indian tribe that lived in the region and was part of the Sioux Indian nation. Springfield was founded by John Polk Campbell in 1829. He donated fifty acres of land on which to begin construction of the town in 1836. Springfield became incorporated as a city in 1838. The Missouri Pacific Railroad was the first railroad to cross the Mississippi River, traveling along the southern portion of the state and running through the city. The St. Louis & San Francisco Railroad established its headquarters there, giving the town a major connection to the western reaches of the country.

The city named many of its streets after famous American heroes, such as General Ulysses S. Grant, General John Fremont, and Presidents Washington and Jefferson. The county was named after General Nathaniel Greene, who was a famous Revolutionary War general. Springfield has its own history of war. The Battle of Wilson's Creek occurred just west of town in 1861, which was the first major battle of the Civil War west of the Mississippi River. It was won by the Confederates. In 1863, a second Battle of Springfield was fought closer to the center of town. The Union forces took permanent control of the region after the Confederates retreated from their superior forces.

The only famous event that occurred in Springfield was the shootout between Wild Bill Hickok and his friend Davis Tutt. The story handed down was that Hickok lost all his money and his pocket watch to Tutt in a poker game held in the Kelly Kerr Saloon on the town square in July 1865. Tutt bragged that he was going to wear Wild Bill's watch and tell everyone about how he had beaten Wild Bill in the card game. Hickok warned him not to wear the watch in public or he would have to kill him.

The following day, word was out that Tutt was walking around town waving the watch in the air. He was not one to back down to a threat, and he knew he was the better gunfighter. Tutt waited for Hickok to show up since the town was buzzing about a possible gunfight and he was sure Hickok had heard about it. The two men squared off about seventy-five yards apart, and, drawing first, Tutt fired, missing Hickok's left ear by inches. The bullet from Wild Bill's gun hit Tutt in the chest, killing him on the spot. There was a trial, but it didn't last long because so many people witnessed the fight and testified that Tutt drew first. The legend of Wild Bill Hickok began right there in Springfield's town square. The city has been a quiet place ever since.

Stephen and Michael attended Jarrett Junior High School, which was about a mile south of the center of town. They were typical young men who attended church and Sunday school every week and most Wednesday night prayer services. Mom's family was from a small town near Ozark called Mentor, where they were raised devout Baptist. She continued the same religious upbringing with the boys. Mom was strict but not too strict.

The boys were turning out to be fine young men. They loved their school and their friends, but they loved their vacations even more. Springfield would get snow every year, but that year the snow was frequent and heavy. There were some great snowball fights, homemade snow ice cream, and hot chocolate. But the best thing about this day was the hockey game, and nothing stood in the way of winning the first battle of the season.

During winter and summer, the boys spent most of their time outdoors. Springfield had almost everything a kid could want. There were forests for hunting and hiking, lakes for fishing and skiing, caves for exploring, and organized sports at school for football, basketball, and baseball. Last month, the boys' basketball team was selected to play a game at the United States Medical Center for Federal Prisoners on the southwest side of town. Robert Stroud, the Birdman of Alcatraz, was in the crowd watching the game, as were many other organized crime figures. Once each summer, Dad would take them to see a Cardinals baseball game in St. Louis. Winter had hockey and basketball, but the summers had baseball and skiing.

The Porter family had a cabin on Table Rock Lake, and, during the summer, they went to the lake two or three times a month for fishing and water sports. They would get up before sunrise to get the bass boat ready for launch. Dad and the boys would fish until late morning. The afternoon was for skiing. All year round, the family was active in sports, school, and church activities. It was a great place to raise a family.

Gilbert Porter was just finishing his breakfast and leaving for work. He owned a Texaco gas station near the center of town. He went to work early and came home late six days a week. He never worked on Sunday because that was the Lord's Day. Mr. Porter was also raised by strict parents who saw many challenges in raising a family during the Depression. To help make ends meet at home on the farm, Gilbert Porter joined the US Navy during the war and sent some of his extra money home each month to help his parents. While in the service, he learned the mechanic's trade and opened a gas station and automotive repair business in Springfield after the war. Eventually, his parents moved from Ozark to Springfield, and Gilbert's father began working at the gas station as well. He named it Gilbert's Gas.

Dad kissed Mom good-bye and wished the boys good luck in their game as he headed out the door. Christmas had brought the boys new skates and sticks. The excitement was palpable as they retrieved their hoods, masks, coats, and gloves from the closet. Hockey season was only about four weeks long and only if the weather obliged. There was no time to waste. Finally, Pat got fitted with his sweater and booties for his paws, and out into the frigid tundra they went.

Chapter Two

The boys set out to find their friends on the way to the lake. The bright blue, cloudless sky gave a feeling of warmth to the deep, fresh snow from the night before. The cold wind began to bite through the ski masks the boys wore, but nothing could dampen their spirit. It was such a beautiful sight as they strolled past Portland Elementary School behind KYTV Channel 3 television station, moving west toward Elfindale Lake.

Springfield was covered in a blanket of thick snow that had been there for more than a week. Due to the amount of snow, the streets were vacant each evening over Christmas. This made for some fun as Dad would hitch the boys' sleds to his Ford station wagon and pull them through the neighborhood. Sometimes their friends would join in, and Dad would have seven or eight sleds connected at once. There seemed to be no end to the fun and excitement the snow brought.

It was a thirty-minute walk to Elfindale. Along the way, they gathered their friends, who were gripped with anticipation of the first hockey game of the season. Within an hour, they had rounded up eight more players. Gary, Stan, Phillip, Keith, Danny, Tom, Richard, and Chuck were all ready and waiting for the boys to come by and accompany them to the ice. They were all experienced skaters and had participated in the hockey matches for the past two years. Most of the guys had gotten new skates for Christmas and were anxious to try them out. The walk to the ice was filled with chatter about their

Christmas gifts and how great the rest of the week would be. They planned to have a hockey game every day until school started after the New Year.

Finally they reached Elfindale, which was a one-hundred-acre property owned by the Catholic Sisters of the Visitation from St. Louis and purchased in 1906. They established the Saint de Chantal Academy of the Visitation, which was a boarding and day school for girls. The previous owners of the property had built a beautiful stone mansion to which the Sisters added a residence for the priest and the Our Lady of the Visitation Chapel. If the stories were true, the Sisters were a very mean and strict bunch of old women. The school building, which was quite old, was a three-story structure built in stone with ornate window treatments that gave the impression of a dungeon. The large front doors were mostly of glass, which allowed you to peer into the main hall. Situated about thirty feet from the front doors sat a tall, hand-carved wooden chair. Legend was that chair was where they tied the girls up and whipped them for breaking the school rules, such as not making it to morning prayers or being caught kissing a boy. It was a foreboding place that you always avoided unless it was closed for the holidays.

About two hundred yards from the school was the lake on the southwest corner of the property. It was surrounded by weeping willow trees whose branches were long and swayed with the wind. It was the most beautiful and peaceful place the boys had ever seen. The only sound they could hear was the wind. Its beauty was admired by all during both winter and summer. The lake was about one hundred yards across at its widest point and was just the perfect size for hockey. The boys quickly began marking the ice for the out-of-bounds lines and the goals. The goals were made from wooden posts that formed the frames. Burlap netting was strung on the back of the frames, and bags of sand held them in place. Once the field was marked, the boys laced up their skates and began choosing teams.

There were two sets of brothers, Spud and Spike and Richard and Chuck. Each would select their own team members, which would make teams of five each, four skaters and one goalie on each team. Spike, Spud, Gary, Tom, and Phillip were on one team, and Richard, Chuck, Danny, Keith, and Stan were on the other. Phillip and Stan were the goalies. Pat would be the equipment manager, which meant that he would retrieve the errant puck whenever needed. Pat was also the lookout in case any of the nuns showed up unexpectedly. All was set, and the game was to begin.

The game was divided into three periods of thirty minutes each. To begin the game, the puck was placed in the center of the field, and one player from each team stood over it. At the signal, usually a bark from Pat, they would fight for control. The faceoff was accompanied by a loud crack from the hockey sticks as the season officially opened.

The puck popped out in the direction of Stephen, who controlled it and shoved it off to Michael. He passed it to Tom, and they headed toward the defenders at the other end of the rink. Tom gave a passing shot to Gary, who had a shot on goal, but it was taken away by Chuck. He shoved it off to Danny, and back down the ice they went. It took a while for the boys to regain their skating prowess as a large number of falls and head-on crashes into the goals occurred. But that was a big part of the fun.

The teams battled into the second period before anyone scored. Finally, Richard took a pass from Danny, and his shot on goal was good, right between Phillip's legs. As the game progressed, all the players became more skilled at skating and handling the puck after the long layoff since last winter. They were enjoying every minute of it. After the first two periods, the game was tied 2–2.

The third period would be the hardest fought of all. With only twelve minutes left in the game, Richard fired on goal and just missed. His puck flew just right of the net and out of bounds. Pat took off to retrieve the puck, and the boys called time-out to rest up for a while before finishing the game. They sat on the ice and talked about their Christmas gifts and plans for the holiday. They also relived some of the events of the game and the great shots on goal. After a few minutes, the boys realized that Pat had not returned with the puck. Spud got up to find him and left the others sitting on the sideline planning their strategy for the rest of the match. You can bet the last few minutes would be intense.

Suddenly, they were interrupted by Spud's screams. Pat was in trouble and needed help. As the boys jumped up and skated across the lake, they saw Pat struggling in the water. He had fallen through the ice about forty feet from the bank and was trying as best he could to climb back onto the slippery edge. Unfortunately, he was unable to get a grip on the edge of the ice. There was no time to lose. Spud got belly-down on the ice and crawled out to within a few feet of the ice edge. He thought he could grab Pat's collar and pull him up. The others would help by forming a human chain, each one holding onto the ankles of the one in front of them. So they all went down on the ice, and Spike grabbed Spud's ankles, and Richard grabbed Spike's ankles, and so on until they were sure they had each other in a firm grip. Slowly, they crawled out so that Spud could grab Pat's collar. After a minute or so, Spud was able to grasp the thick, leather collar, and he began to slowly retreat from the edge while dragging Pat with him.

Spud had Pat nearly out of the water onto the edge of the ice when, suddenly, the area around Spud began to crack. Everyone stopped in panic. The silence filled each boy with fear. Maybe it was just a small crack and nothing more would happen. So the small group of hockey players waited until the sound stopped. Spike told Spud to let Pat go and they would try another way to get him out of the water, but Spud would not let go.

"I'm the only one who can save him, and I have a good grip on him."

They decided to try again and the human chain slowly advanced. Suddenly, thousands of tiny, cracking sounds were audible as the ice developed the appearance of a huge spider web. In one terrifying moment, the ice gave way in a loud, dreadful sound like breaking glass. Now both Spud and Pat were in the water holding each other in terror. With no time to lose, Spike told Keith to run for help while the others came up with a plan. They tore the burlap from the goals and tied the hockey sticks together, making a lifeline to throw out to Spud. The whole process took several minutes, during which time the cold was making it difficult for Spud to swim and hoist Pat above the frigid water.

The lifeline was completed and stretched about twenty feet. They threw the line to Spud, who grabbed it with one hand and with the other grasped the thick collar around Pat's neck. The fighting and thrashing was intense. Spud could not get a grip on the slippery ice and kept falling back into the water. Within minutes, Spud's efforts to remain afloat began to slow as his muscles were being paralyzed by the frigid water. In spite of all his efforts, Spud's strength was gone. Spike pleaded with him to let Pat go and let them save him, but Spud refused. He would not be responsible for letting Pat drown.

The battle waged for what seemed like an eternity, and the freezing temperatures took their toll. They could no longer fight to stay afloat, and slowly both Spud and Pat disappeared below the surface. The boys stared in shocked disbelief.

This was not supposed to happen! This was supposed to be fun! they thought.

A deathly, cold silence encircled the group as Spike began to cry. It was like a large part of his soul had been ripped out and thrown into the bottom of the lake. There was nothing they could do. Spud and Pat were gone. Out of the silence came a distant siren. The rescue team was fighting the heavy snow in a vain attempt to get there in time.

It took two hours for the rescue squad to find their bodies. By the time Spud's parents arrived, other parents were already there consoling the boys. The local television station, KYTV 3, was just a few blocks away and had sent a reporter and film crew to cover the tragedy. It would be the lead story on the ten o'clock news for the next three days. But there was no consoling Spike. His dearest friend and brother were gone, and there was no going back. His life and that of his parents would never be the same. The winter snow would never be the same either.

The stricken family returned home to find the entire neighborhood standing around their house. Everyone was offering their help in any way they could. Some families were going to help with meals, and others would help handle the many phone calls that had already started to come in. Mr. Porter's best friend was there, and he would represent the family in statements made to the television and radio reporters that were gathering on the street in front of the house.

The next six hours was a total blur to the Porter family. Pastor McDowell arrived and met with the family for about an hour. He said he would handle the necessary arrangements for the memorial service and help them with the funeral and burial plans. One of the church deacons would come by the next day to accompany them to the funeral home and help them get through this ordeal.

All of the necessary arrangements were being made, but no one could comfort Spike. *This is not supposed to happen to kids on Christmas vacation. It's not supposed to happen to your brother. What am I supposed to do now?* he thought. No one had an answer.

ELFINDALE, SPRINGFIELD, MO.

Chapter Three

No one knows the happiness or sorrow a day will bring forth. Certainly no one thought this would be how they would spend their Christmas vacation. It is Tuesday, December 29, 1959, and the three previous days challenged the sanity of the whole family. Visitation was held the previous evening at the funeral home. There were faces filled with sorrow, grown men with tears in their eyes, and very few words spoken as the friends and family gathered to say good-bye to one of their own. Not only were there friends from school, church, and the neighborhood, but there were people from the community that didn't even know Spud but came to pay their respects. The horrible tragedy seemed to grip everyone in Springfield, both young and old.

The same year that the boys were born, their mother lost a brother in WWII. He was a navy pilot and was lost at sea in the Pacific Ocean. She also lost a sister to illness one year later. But having the two boys seemed to help her maintain her sanity during that awful time right after the war. The tragedy of Christmas 1959 seemed to bring back the painful emotions of grief and loss that gripped her life. She was so weak from the enormous burden she carried that Gilbert had to help hold her up as she greeted all those in attendance.

The funeral and graveside services seemed to signal the beginning of the loss they would feel for a very long time. Maple Park Cemetery was near the center of town and could be seen from the three-story schoolhouse where Spike would have to return next week. It was a beautiful place in summer. The lawns were deep green and always well-trimmed. Hundreds of mature maple, oak, elm, and hickory trees filled the cemetery and provided shade to the thousands of tombstones placed there. Now it was a cold and desolate place, a place Spike would pass every day he went to school for the next six months.

The funeral service at church was led by Dr. McDowell. All went well as the church filled with mourners to hear the brief sermon. He had always seemed to be a rock during trying times like these and he had to interrupt his sermon twice to fight back his own emotions. After the service, a long line of cars followed the hearse from the church to the cemetery, taking every precaution in the heavy snow outside. The cars lined the narrow paths through the cemetery as far as the eye could see.

As they left their cars and walked to the grave, not a word was spoken. All that could be heard was the crunching of the snow as they walked and the gentle sobs from the family. The sky was overcast, and a gentle mist of cold rain and snow fell. It was as if heaven itself was crying cold, grey tears. Spike was dressed in a new suit Dad bought him for the funeral. He would never wear it again. He had not slept in days and was numb to all feelings except his grief. There was no one consoling him, not that anyone could at that moment.

Stephen and Michael had been to only two funerals before. One was for their grandfather, Edward Porter, who died ten years to the day after his son died in the war. The second one was for their church buddy, Rickey, who died from what the doctor called leukemia. Spike could not take his eyes off the cold, deep hole that had been dug for Spud's last resting place. *Somebody pinch me and wake me up. This can't be happening!* he thought.

The graveside service was brief, and Spike heard not a word. Pastor McDowell read some scriptures and said all the right things, but the deep sorrow he felt was evident on his face. He said Spud was in a better place and that they would all see him again. But these were empty words with little comfort for Spike as he knew he would have to live the rest of his life without his best friend. He would also have to live with the vivid memory of how he died just three days past. How could he go on? How could any of them go on?

Outside the cemetery a KYTV 3 reporter was taping a segment about the tragedy for the evening news:

> We are outside the Maple Park Cemetery, where about one hundred cars have brought friends and family to say good-bye to the son of Mr. and Mrs. Gilbert Porter. The gloomy skies above seem fitting for such a sad day as this because no one expected they would be here during the otherwise joyous Christmas holiday. The danger of ice skating on frozen ponds and lakes has never been more poignant than it is on this day. We will talk to some of those gathered here and get their feelings about this tragedy for you on our 6:00 p.m. newscast. Until then, this is Ellen Clements reporting for KYTV 3 News.

As the service ended, everyone from the family took the white rose that was pinned to their coats and placed it on the silver coffin that sat suspended over the deep hole in the ground. As the coffin was slowly lowered into the ground, the crowd receded and disappeared into the mist and snow that was falling heavily all around them. Spike was left alone as he said good-bye to his brother. He couldn't bear leaving him there in that cold, dark place.

After a few minutes, his dad returned to accompany him back to their car. Instead, they both sat down next to Spud and cried. They cried until the tears wouldn't come anymore. Spike looked up into his father's face and said, "I was the only one who could save him, and I didn't. How can I live with that?"

His father thought for a moment and then whispered into Spike's ear, "You will find throughout your life there will be many friends and family you will want to save, but you will not be able to save them. This is just the way life is sometimes. God doesn't make these things happen; they just happen. God doesn't judge us based on whether bad things happen to us or the mistakes we make. He judges us on how we handle these things when they happen to us. At some time in our lives, they happen to us all. If you handle them the right way, you will become a stronger and more loving person. There will be others you can save."

Father and son sat there in silence for a while. Then they slowly got up and walked away. As they were leaving, Spike looked back to see the cemetery attendants begin their job of shoveling dirt into the grave.

The tears came back.

Chapter Four

It is Tuesday evening, September 15, 1970, and Gentle Ben's Bar & Bistro just opened. The first two weeks of the month had been the busiest Ben had seen in the eight months since his new business enterprise began. He converted an old coin shop and the adjacent children's toy store on South Street, near the town square, into a modern bar and restaurant that specialized in beer and barbeque.

The downtown area was in need of a good dining establishment since most of the fast-food ventures were opening on Glenstone Street to the east and Sunshine Street to the south of town. Springfield was centered in the geographic and population center of the country, making it a prime location for franchise eateries to test the market. Ben's place served the community interested in a neighborhood-style bar and grill. He wanted one that was situated between the upscale steak houses on one end and the fast-food outlets at the other end of the spectrum. Now that his clientele was blossoming, he was considering opening for lunch as well.

Benjamin Edward Melton had wanted to have his own restaurant for many years. This town was where he was born and where he grew up. He was a tall, well-built, young man who was a star athlete at Parkview High School and helped win the school's 1965 State Basketball Championship. After high school, he enlisted in the Marine Corps and did a four-year stint in Vietnam.

During his tour, he saw firsthand how much evil men could do to others. There were men maimed for life and men who suffered long before their death in that faraway jungle of Southeast Asia. He also saw a great deal of heroism in his fellow soldiers. Ben was shot while rescuing his buddy that had been wounded as his platoon was crossing an open field. The Viet Cong had them pinned down for over an hour when Ben decided it was time to act. He picked his friend up out of the mud and carried him over three hundred yards to safety behind some trees. During his dash to safety, Ben was hit by a bullet that punctured his left lung. He spent six weeks in a naval hospital aboard the *USS Forrestal* aircraft carrier before he could return to action. For this act of bravery, he was awarded the Purple Heart. Ben preferred not to talk about the war, so it was not a topic of conversation in the bar. His buddy survived and is now a minister in a church in Tulsa, Oklahoma. It is amazing how things turn out sometimes.

After his return, he took some of the money he received from his late father's estate and opened the bar. The competition in Springfield was tough, but Ben was not known for backing down from a fight, and, so far, the venture was a success. Soon after opening, there had been some customers who thought getting drunk and starting a bar fight was the way to have fun. Ben managed to teach them a valuable lesson on decency, one they would never forget. The word around town was Ben's Bar was not the place to start trouble. Gentle Ben's Bar & Bistro was just what the sign said, a gentle and comfortable place to be for great BBQ and beer.

The bar quickly filled that evening, and the suds and hot wings were moving well. The atmosphere was quite comfortable for mid-September, with temperatures in the sixties during the day and the forties at night. The city was home to several colleges. The largest was Southwest Missouri State, followed by Drury College, Evangel College, Baptist Bible College, and the Assemblies of God Theological Seminary. The college crowd, which consisted mostly of the SMS and Drury students, was always there when the doors opened, and some were still there when they closed. The restaurant was open six days a week but never on Sunday. That was the Lord's Day. A large number of patrons came from downtown stores as well as from the police department and the courthouse. Gentle Ben's was the place to be and the place to be seen.

The front door opened, and Lillian Rooney walked in. She was a regular at the bar and would frequently stop by for a brew after work. Rooney, as her friends called her, was a family law attorney with an office near the courthouse a few blocks north of the bar. She was quite attractive but dedicated to her work and not interested in settling down with anyone at the moment. When she was ready, she would not have to look far for male suitors. Rooney was born in Arkansas and graduated from Drury College in prelaw. She received her law degree from the University of Arkansas in Little Rock and became an associate of a local law firm. Her long, auburn hair was always rolled up in back and tied with a ribbon. She was wearing a dark brown executive suit with black pumps on her feet. She had brains, and she had looks. Rooney seemed to light up the room every time she came into Ben's.

Accompanying Rooney was her best friend, Patti Jo Dickinson. Her friends called her PJ. She was a looker as well. PJ was taller than Rooney with short, black hair and had a rather forceful personality. They had met at Drury when they joined the same sorority. After PJ graduated, she got her law degree from the University of Missouri in Columbia. She moved back to Springfield and joined a real estate law firm. PJ was married to Russell, a Drury basketball coach and a star player himself at Drury a few years ago. She was an accomplished violinist and played with the Springfield Symphony.

Both ladies were still active alumni of Drury. The institution had been an important part of the city since its inception in 1873. A group known as the Congregational Home Missionaries felt the need for an institution of higher learning in the city that offered a liberal arts education with special emphasis on religion and music. The college was patterned after other Congregationalist colleges of the north, such as Yale, Dartmouth, and Harvard. One of the four prominent citizens who organized and endowed the college was Mr. Samuel Drury from Otsego, Michigan. Since his donation to the institution was the largest, he was given the honor of naming the new college. It was named Drury in honor of his son who had recently passed away. The first classes were held on September 25, 1873, on a small plot of land about one and one-half acres. The campus quickly grew to forty acres and remained so for most of the life of the college. Even though the campus was over ninety acres in size now, it is still affectionately referred to by the alumni as "The Forty Acres" of Drury College.

Rooney and PJ moved to open seats at the bar.

"What can I get for you, ladies?" asked Ben.

"Two Budweiser's please."

Rooney and PJ loved to talk about the law. Their whole life was dedicated to practicing law, and most other aspects of their lives took a backseat. They would talk about their cases, their clients, opposing attorneys, as well as the most unusual people they would meet. PJ had an appointment earlier that day with an elderly farmer who felt the Springfield Regional Airport had illegally taken over a portion of his farm during a recent expansion. His farm had been in his family for over a century, and the boundary lines were very difficult to obtain accurately. This man came to the office wearing overalls and leather work boots covered in something she tried to ignore. For thirty minutes, he described his concerns in great detail and asked for her help. He was a quiet man, very polite and unassuming. What PJ found out was that this old farmer owned six thousand acres of prime real estate and was one of the wealthiest men in the state. First impressions can be deceiving sometimes.

After a few minutes, Rooney noticed music coming from the back room of the bar. There hadn't been any music at Gentle Ben's before, and it sounded terrific. She had seen the piano in the back dining area that Ben had been using as a plant stand. No one knew it even worked.

"Hey, Ben! How about some chicken wings? Put the barbeque sauce on the side, would you?" Within minutes, the best hot, steamy, BBQ chicken wings she had ever tasted were placed under her nose.

"You got a new sound system in here?" asked PJ.

"Well, sort of," he answered. "Three days ago, this fellow comes into the bar and noticed I had that old piano in the back. It's an old Baldwin console piano that was left here when I bought the place. I kept it because it added some ambiance to the room, but no one ever played it. He asked me if he could play, and I said sure! It was out of tune, but within an hour, he had it tuned up and began to play. Let me tell you, this guy can play. He knows all the songs of the Beatles, The Beach Boys, Sam Cooke, Motown, Elvis, you name it. Matter of fact, you can ask him to play any tune, and he knows them all. No one has stumped him yet. Long story short, he asked to play for the customers every evening for nothing. That's right, he entertains the customers every night for free except for all the Coca-Cola he wants. So, of course, I said yes, and there he is. Handsome dude but very quiet."

Rooney was fascinated by the story. "So where does he work? Is he a piano teacher? What?"

"Get this!" he replied. "He works for the Humane Society over on Chestnut Trafficway. He takes care of the animals during the day and then plays the piano until we close at 2:00 a.m. The guy seems quite happy about the way things are, but if I had his talent, I'd be on a stage somewhere making the big bucks. In addition to his incredible talent, he doesn't drink alcohol. Not a drop."

Rooney polished off her beer and excused herself from Ben and PJ. "I'm going to take a look at this guy. I'll be back in a minute."

Ben looked at PJ and gave her a wink.

Rooney reached the back room, which had ten or twelve tables, half of which were filled with customers. She stopped and sat down at an empty table and listened to the music.

The mastery of the instrument was readily apparent. There were no missed notes, and he played with such feeling. He played Simon

& Garfunkel, Rare Earth, The Jackson 5, Three Dog Night, The Carpenters, and even some Bach and Beethoven. He was so into the music that he was oblivious to anyone else in the room. After he finished his rendition of "When a Man Loves a Woman," first recorded by Percy Sledge, she walked over and sat down on the piano bench next to him.

"Do you know 'In My Life' by the Beatles?"

Without speaking or looking up at her, he began to play. It was not exactly like the Beatles did it. It was better! Sometimes in life, amid the stones you find a diamond. This guy was a diamond. He was in his mid-twenties, handsome, about six feet tall with dark brown hair and eyes. He was dressed in a flannel shirt and blue jeans with a large cowboy belt buckle that seemed somewhat out of place for him. He was very self-assured, and when asked to play another tune, there was no pause to remember the song. It was as if he knew what to play before he was asked.

"Okay, play 'I Can't Take My Eyes Off of You' by Frankie Valli."

Once again, he played the tune as if he were in an opera house on center stage.

"So, where do you perform? I bet you have quite a show," she said as he looked at her.

"Here, just here," he answered.

"I find that hard to believe. My name is Lillian, Lillian Rooney. What's yours?"

"My name is Michael Porter."

"What else do you do, Michael Porter?"

"I work at the Humane Society. I was hired a few weeks ago after I moved back to Springfield from out east. I was born here and was anxious to return, so I did. Taking care of the animals has always been a passion for me, so I hooked up with the city animal shelter. That's what I do. What do you do, Lillian Rooney?"

"I'm an attorney with a family law firm. I was born in Little Rock and graduated from Drury before going to law school at the University of Arkansas."

"Do you like what you do, Lillian?"

"I love what I do. Family law is a very challenging field because we assist our clients with divorces and child custody. Family court can be too exciting at times. Like today, another fight broke out between a man and his wife over a child custody case. It took the bailiff and two policemen to break it up. I was under the table the whole time. Usually, things are under control but not today. But every day is exciting!"

"Well, you can't be too careful nowadays," Michael said with a sigh. "How long have you been a family law attorney?"

"About two years now. Every day has new challenges, but I love what I do."

"Me, too! How about another song?"

"You pick one you think I would like, and then I have to head home!" she answered.

Michael played "Close to You" by The Carpenters, and a hush fell over the room. No rattling of dinnerware and no conversation as everyone was mesmerized by the music. Rooney just sat there as if in another world.

When he finished, Rooney said, "Okay, one more, and then I really have to head home."

After a brief pause, Michael said, "Here's one I think is beautiful and it probably fits you." Then he began to play and sing.

Ain't no sunshine when she's gone
It's not warm when she's away
Ain't no sunshine when she's gone
She's always gone too long anytime she goes away

Wonder this time where she's gone
Wonder if she's gone to stay
Ain't no sunshine when she's gone
This house just ain't no home anytime she goes away.

The small crowd loved it, and so did Rooney. Several of the women had tears in their eyes by the time he finished.

Rooney found it incredible to see someone so talented and yet so kind and shy. He could make a fortune with his talent but didn't seem interested in that in the least. He was truly a unique person, and Rooney was sure there was more to the story about him.

"It's been very nice meeting you, and I wish I could stay longer, but I've got to head home. I'll see you again, I'm sure," she said as she rose from the bench.

"I'm sure you will," he replied.

Standing behind her with a tear in her eye and astonishment on her face was PJ. As they walked together from the room, she whispered into Rooney's ear, "And this guy is a dog catcher?"

Chapter Five

The courthouse opened at 8:00 the next morning. In preparation for her 9:00 court session with Judge Hal Sandrotas, Ms. Rooney had arrived early to make copies of legal documents for opposing counsel in a child-support hearing. Most of these cases were settled before court, and the litigants came to court with an agreement in hand. However, they needed to be presented to the court in open session. The judge had to pronounce the final judgment or settlement before the decision could be entered into the court records. All cases on the docket for the day that were adjudicated were entered into the court records and published within twenty-four hours in the *Springfield News and Leader* newspaper. Those decisions were a matter of public record unless information was suppressed by the judge. The process ran smoothly many times a day throughout the state.

There are twelve family law attorneys and four family law judges in the Thirty-First Judicial Circuit for Greene County. The court system was similar from state to state with each state having several levels to the system. The highest court was the State Supreme Court. Under the Supreme Court are the appellate courts. In Missouri, there are three appellate courts, which are found in St. Louis, Kansas City, and Springfield, the three largest cities in the state. Under the appellate courts are the circuit courts, which are divided into municipal courts and specialized courts. It was under the specialized courts that the family courts and juvenile courts are located.

Any decision by the circuit courts could be appealed to a higher court. It was up to the appellate court judges whether or not they would hear the case brought before them. The family law division operated the same in all 114 counties of Missouri. The system ran very well, and the judges and attorneys were dedicated to their mission of settling family disputes and protecting the children involved.

The case before the court that day involved a defendant father who had not made his child-support payments for the past six months and was charged with contempt of court. The earlier court decision was for him to pay $200 per month for child support, but he was in arrears for $1,200. Judge Sandrotas came into court, and the court session was called to order at exactly 9:00.

"Ms. Rooney, I see you are counsel for the plaintiff. Please begin."

Lillian Rooney began her summary of the particulars of the case for which the judge had issued the contempt charge. The matter was very straight forward, and the case summary was brief and to the point. Judge Sandrotas was a man who wanted just the necessary facts presented, and he did not tolerate grandstanding by the attorneys. He also wanted all documents to be on his desk when they were due, and he expected everyone to be dressed appropriately when in his court. He once put a man in jail for two days because he came to court in Bermuda shorts.

On completion of her summary, the judge asked the opposing counsel to respond. The attorney for the defendant, Mr. Jamieson, stated their only defense in the matter was that the defendant was currently unemployed and had no money to make the payments. They asked the court for its consideration of this difficult situation that was preventing him from complying. Judge Sandrotas was a considerate man who ruled his court with common sense and decency. Before going forward in this matter, he required a meeting in his chambers with both attorneys to discuss the issues involved. Once the attorneys were seated in front of his desk, he let it be known that the previous court ruling required that the defendant pay the monthly support regardless of his predicament of being unemployed.

"My only option is to incarcerate the man for seven days for contempt of court, but it would not assist the child or her mother for him to be locked up. So I am anxious for you two to suggest to me how we can work this out. He needs to come up with the $1,200 somehow. Does he have anything he can sell? Does he have family that would be interested in helping him come up with the money?

"Don't come to my court again without providing potential solutions and then expect me to bail you out, no pun intended. Now, I have another case at 10:00, forty-seven minutes from now. You do not have much time. However, you both have had months to correct this problem before bringing it to my court. You are excused for now, and I want you back here in half an hour with my solution or you may be found in contempt!"

The judge was correct in his assessment of the situation. It was the attorneys' responsibility to help solve this problem, and sending the man to jail was not the answer. After informing the man and his wife about their meeting, Ms. Rooney and Mr. Jamieson each found a phone and started making calls. They called every business where they knew the employers. They called anyone that owed them a favor and even considered hiring the man themselves. They were having no luck, and time was short.

The secretary at Mr. Jamieson's office recalled that a friend of her son had signed on to a new company that arranged day workers for five dollars an hour. The company was called DayWork, Inc. All you had to do was show up at their offices downtown at 6:00 every morning, and they would assign a position for you to work that day. Most of the industries in the city participated with DayWork because they all, from time to time, would have an employee absent and needed a temporary replacement. It meant you could make $40 a day, but it did not include any benefits. Those who were unemployed and wanted work were given a new job every day, and companies who needed a day laborer could always find their temporary replacements through DayWork. Most days, everyone who wanted to work got placed somewhere, and the company van transported them to the work site. It was a win-win situation.

They presented the plan to Judge Sandrotas after receiving an agreement from the defendant. If he did not comply, he would be incarcerated. He was so appreciative for their help because he truly wanted to make good on his support payments but felt helpless to do so. The attorneys formulated a plan of repayment of the debt over the next twelve weeks while remaining current on all payments due each month. Court was called back into session, where the judge announced his decision for the record. He also gave a stern warning to all parties that his concern was for the welfare of the child. If any problems were to develop in the future, he expected them to handle them without wasting time in his court. He chastised the attorneys for letting this violation of the previous court order go on for so long and fully expected it would not happen again.

Judge Sandrotas could be very stern in court and in chambers, but at the end of the day, he was someone you could have a beer with and talk baseball, fishing, or the law. However, any lesson given in court must be learned and never forgotten. His concern was always for the children who had no effective voice of their own in these personal matters of family disputes. At the end of the day, all was well if the children were provided for both financially and emotionally with meaningful time each week with both parents. Today was a good day, and Rooney was proud to be a part of family court.

"Mr. Jamieson, how about a beer after work?" Rooney asked with a sly grin as court was adjourned.

"You're on! See you at Ben's about 5:30," he replied.

Rooney had three other cases later that day, all of which were routine and only required her to submit documents requested by the court. Last of all, there was a mediation set up at 4:00 p.m. to determine monthly support for a plaintiff wife prior to divorce court, which was scheduled for the following March. Hopefully, Rooney would be able to find a divorce settlement, which would prevent her from having to draw the case out until then. If you go to court, you never know what might happen. The case load had definitely increased the past month, as it usually did after the summer. All in all, the day was productive, and off to Ben's she went. Maybe she would get to see Michael again.

"Evening, Ben, how are you doing?" she inquired as she snuggled up to the bar.

"Everything is just fine. How about a Bud?" Ben asked with a broad smile. He enjoyed having Rooney at the bar. She attracted more customers than anyone else.

"Works for me! Is Michael here?"

"Oh, yeah! He comes in at opening every night like clockwork."

Rooney grabbed her beer and told Ben to be on the lookout for Mr. Jamieson. "Set him up with a beer and put it on my tab, would you? And let him know I'm in the back."

She danced off to the back room, where Michael was busy with several people standing around the piano making him work for his money or, rather, his Coca-Cola. Everyone had a request for him to play, and without missing a beat, he played them all. After he had played a few songs, he asked them to let him take a break so he could consult with his attorney.

"Consult with your attorney?" Rooney said, giving him a soft elbow to the ribs. "I didn't know you needed an attorney. Are you getting a divorce? I can help you with that."

"No, I'm not married. Fortunately, I have no need for legal counsel at the moment."

"Well, that's good to know!" Actually she was referring to the "not married" part.

"Tell me, where did you study the piano?" she asked.

"When I was in school, they had a piano in the music room where they kept all the marching band equipment. The music instructor, Mr.

Palen, was a terrific piano player, and I admired his talent. So I started learning the chords and playing some tunes after school. Soon after that, my mom got me a piano for my own. I took lessons for many years and loved music almost as much as sports."

"You're kidding me?"

"Nope! I'm serious. I just loved playing the piano. It's fun to play for people who appreciate good music without having to buy a ticket. But I'm not interested in making it my vocation. Life shouldn't be complicated, and that would definitely complicate mine. My first love is working with the animals. Hey, you should come by the shelter and see the place. I'll bet you'll be amazed at what you see."

"Well, Michael Porter, you are a rare breed, indeed! Okay, let me see if I can stump you. If I can, you have to buy me a Coca-Cola. If I can't, I'll have to come over to the animal shelter to see where you work and what you do there. Is that a deal?"

"That's a deal!"

"Play me 'I Can't Help Falling In Love.' Elvis sang that song in the movie *Blue Hawaii*, and I have always loved it."

No sooner had the words fallen from her lips than Michael began to play. For a brief time, Rooney was lost in the melody. She had never met anyone who could play the piano so well, play anything she wanted, and he seemed so out of place there in the back of a bar. It was a nice bar, but it was still just a bar.

"That was beautiful! Well, I guess I'll have to come by tomorrow so you can give me a tour. Would that be all right?"

"Sure, that would be swell!"

"I should be free late in the morning, and I'll call you before I come over."

Michael gave her the number as she left to meet Mr. Jamieson at the bar.

Jamieson was an older gentleman who had been in family law a very long time. He was one of the few that really wanted what was best for the family at large and not just for his clients. He took care in explaining his position to them. Even though the family was separated, he was still interested in having both parents cooperate for the best possible outcome for the children involved. Rooney felt the same way, and she appreciated her relationship with attorneys who had the same dedication. They enjoyed their beer and conversation while hot wings and BBQ sandwiches flew around the room.

"Ben, when are you going to open for lunch?"

"The way things are going, it may not be too far away."

"Good for you, Ben! Good for you."

Greene County Court House, Springfield, Mo.

Chapter Six

Rooney had Thursday morning off and wasn't due to be in court until 2:00 with Judge Holt for a preliminary divorce hearing. She called the shelter and reached Michael, who was cleaning the cat cages.

"Hey, this is Rooney. How about I come by at 11:00 for that tour?"

"That would be a good time. I should be finished with my cats by then."

"Great, see you soon."

Rooney was not one to get involved with anyone romantically, although she did have a few dates now and then. But this man really intrigued her. His story, or the little she knew of his story, just didn't make sense to her. He seemed out of place. Outwardly, he did seem quite content with his life the way it was. He was very handsome and quite talented. Maybe he just wasn't motivated to change. It wasn't her place to suggest a change of situation for him or anyone else, but he should be married and recording music, playing concerts, and enjoying life. It was a good idea to meet him at the shelter, and maybe she would find out more about what made him tick. She had a few errands to run and would meet Michael before lunch.

Rooney arrived at the shelter a little early, so she took a few minutes to read over some legal documents she was to submit in court that afternoon. She was interrupted by a knock on her window. It was Michael.

"I thought I saw you drive in. You ready to see the place?"

"Sure. Let me store these papers in the trunk."

Michael took her by the arm and escorted her into the front office of the Humane Society. He was dressed in blue jeans, boots, and a brown Humane Society shirt with a dog and cat image sewn into the left, upper chest. He was clean shaven, and his dark brown hair was shoulder length and combed straight back. He had a square jaw, and he smelled great in spite of working around the animals all day.

He introduced her to Vickie, the receptionist, who was a heavyset woman with a pleasant smile and demeanor. As they entered the kennel, Rooney noticed the faint smell of the dogs, not at all like she thought it would be.

All the dogs seemed to see Michael at the same time as they began to bark and stand up on their hind legs, scratching the cage doors. The animals were clean and, by the wagging of their tails, seemed to be gentle. Every cage was spotless and had two bowls, one for water and one for their food. It would soon be time for lunch and they all knew it. There were about fifty dogs and around eighty cats.

Michael loved them all but was partial to the dogs. He took a German shepherd out of his cage and let "Butch" meet Rooney. He licked her hand and rubbed up against her with his shoulder, expecting to be petted. Michael grabbed a Frisbee, and off they went into the half-acre backyard to play. For about fifteen minutes, they played, and not once did Butch miss catching the Frisbee in midair. Once Butch was worn out, Michael walked him back to his cage and with just a wave of his hand, the dog when into the cage and sat down. He loved those animals, and it showed.

"Most of our dogs were found roaming around neighborhoods, but a few of them had been abused. Some we had to take from their owners. I have never understood why someone would abuse an animal whose only desire in life is to be loved and cared for. When

37

they come to the shelter, we nurse them back to health and teach them to trust us again. The process takes a few months, but I have never found one that couldn't be saved physically and emotionally. We spay or neuter all our animals, and we never euthanize them. Our mission is to find them a loving home only after the animal has been rehabilitated.

"Our facility is one of the best in the country. We have a pharmacy, operating room, boarding kennel, and we have someone onsite 24/7 to watch out for them. Part of my job is to go out to schools and church groups to tell them about our mission. We also ask them to help us by bringing animals they have found, to volunteer their time, or make financial donations to allow us to provide these services. Once they see our facility, they always want to help."

As they walked down the rows of cages, Rooney saw cocker spaniels, dachshunds, poodles, Great Danes, German shepherds, collies, Labradors, and beagles. When they reached the last cage, Michael stopped and opened the door. Inside, lying down on his carpet bed was a huge, brown dog with long, droopy ears and the saddest eyes Rooney had ever seen.

"Come out here, Blue!" Michael demanded. Blue slowly lifted his body up and lumbered out the door. "This is Blue. Don't ask me why a brown dog was named Blue, but I would guess it was because he always seems sad by the look on his face. Blue is my best friend, and we sit and talk to each other every day. There have been a few people who wanted to adopt Blue, but he demands a special kind of owner, and I haven't seen anyone yet who fits the bill. I found Blue in the Appalachian Mountains last year. His care had been ignored by his owner who was quite ill and didn't ask anyone for help. I arranged for him to go to a nursing home in western North Carolina, and he asked me to take his dog and care for him. I was happy to do it, and I brought Blue with me to Springfield. He's a great dog, and we get along quite well."

Rooney reached down and petted Blue on the top of his head but without any change in his demeanor. He just seemed so sad and withdrawn. "Why is Blue your best friend?" she asked.

"Blue has a very important and amazing talent. My talent is music, and his talent is sniffing. Now, that may not seem like a very big deal to most people, but bloodhounds like Blue can smell things you can't smell. His sense of smell is much more advanced than humans, and it makes him ideal for finding things. When Blue is on the hunt, his whole attitude changes. If he's asked to find a lost child in the woods, he's no longer this sad-looking canine but becomes an energetic, tireless, highly motivated investigator for finding whatever you ask him to find. If someone comes here to see Blue, he can still identify their scent two weeks after they leave. I find that simply amazing! But all my animals are amazing in one way or another. I'm just partial to Blue," he said as he rubbed Blue's neck and ears, directing him back to his cage.

Next they toured the infirmary, where the injured animals were given medical treatment. The center of the space looked like an operating room in St. John's Hospital. There were glass cabinets for supplies, an operating room table with a ceiling-mounted light source, and a fully stocked medicine chest for drugs used to anesthetize the animals for surgery or for pain relief after the surgery. The room was spotless, and no surgery was planned for that day. Michael led Rooney into an adjacent room filled with cages for post-op patients or for animals being treated for illness or injury. In one cage was a beagle that was quite emaciated and had bandages on its front legs. Next to it was a cage with a German shepherd that had been beaten by its owner and was being treated for infected wounds. Several cages housed cats that had been in fights with other animals. Local veterinarians came by the shelter daily to check on the patients. It was obvious that the shelter was providing the best care that could be given to these animals. Rooney was totally amazed by what she saw.

"I had a dog when I was young," Rooney said as they returned to the kennel. "But now I'm gone so much during the day with no one to help me look after a dog that I just haven't gotten one for myself. These animals are so beautiful, and thank you for showing them to me. I promise I'm going to volunteer in some way to help in their care," she said as they walked out to her car. "I was not aware of the size and scope of your facility here. The work you do is fabulous! Do you have enough funds to continue to care for these animals?"

"We do, but we could always use more. The shelter account averages about six weeks of funds necessary to provide this level of service, and, fortunately, the vets volunteer their services, which makes it easier for us to function. However, if we have a dramatic increase in animals needing care, we could use up our small nest egg pretty fast. I have begun a program that solicits funds from animal lovers around the city to remember us in their wills. Every little bit helps, and nothing goes to waste. Tell your friends and colleagues about us, or, better yet, bring them over to meet our animals. What we do is a lot like what you do. You're devoted to saving the children, and we're devoted to saving the animals. It's very rewarding what you and I do, don't you think?"

"Yes, I think you're right about that!"

"Hey, how about some lunch?" he asked.

"Sure. What do you have in mind?"

"Let's go by Steak 'n Shake and get some burgers. Then we can go to this park close by and have lunch there."

"Great! Let's go."

"You'll have to drive because I don't have a car," he said, somewhat embarrassed.

"No problem. Hop in!"

The park was located a few blocks north of the Drury College campus and was called Washington Park, presumably after President Washington. It was located in the center of a neighborhood that was frequented by children and, more often than not, their dogs. There were swing sets, slides, merry-go-rounds; all the neat kid stuff.

"I just love to sit here and watch the kids play," Michael said as he spread a blanket from Rooney's car. After setting the burgers and drinks down, they watched the children play as they enjoyed their lunch.

"You seem to have a fascination with animals. Have you always had a love for them, even as a child?" she asked.

"I grew up in south Springfield with my brother and parents. My father owned a Texaco gas station on the corner of Grant and Division Streets downtown. This large dog kept hanging around the station one day. It was a Boston terrier, and he was very friendly. Dad fed him and played with him daily for a week or so. The dog would lie down in his office and take his naps. Dad was afraid a car would run over him at the station, so he brought him home. We named him Pat. Now that I think about it, I have no idea why we named him Pat. That dog became my best friend—next to my brother, of course.

"You know, I just can't imagine a kid growing up without a dog or a cat. It teaches them to care for something that's totally dependent on them and gives them a sense of responsibility. If they learn that lesson well, when they grow up they will be more likely to appreciate life in so many ways. Most importantly, they become more tolerant and loving of other people and this world becomes a better place for us all. Do you agree, Lillian?"

"I certainly do, and I admire you for doing this work," she said with a smile.

"Thanks, I appreciate that. Most people think I'm just a dog catcher. But I'm totally devoted to the animals, and it's very enjoyable to help them out when they are abused or injured."

"Well, I don't think you're a dog catcher. You do this wonderful work, you're very talented, and this world needs more people like you.

I'm glad the animals have you to care for them. What were you doing before you came back to Springfield?" she asked.

"I had an assignment in south Florida for the past year helping to rebuild communities devastated by tropical storms and hurricanes. The storm surge had wiped out most of what was left after the high winds hit the East Coast, and the people there were really hurting."

"How do you get these assignments?"

"I work for a very wealthy philanthropist who gives these assignments to me. He supplies the necessary funding and covers my personal needs while I complete the work. I never know what assignment he'll give me next, which makes it exciting. Right now, my work is with the shelter. Tomorrow it may be feeding and clothing the homeless or fundraising for cancer treatment programs. I never quite know what it will be. I've been to Florida, Dominican Republic, and Mexico for hurricane relief. I have been to Japan for help after an earthquake and spent two years in Africa helping to feed the natives and build wells to pump clean water to their villages. We have also helped to build hospitals in Vietnam to treat those wounded in the war. There is never a dull moment when you do this work, and I feel very lucky to be given this job."

For a while, they just enjoyed the warm September day, watching the kids play. Rooney was amazed how self-assured Michael seemed to be. He never tried to impress her or mislead her about what he truly felt in his heart. He was on a mission, and nothing could stand in his way.

There couldn't be but a few people in the whole world like this guy, she thought.

"Oh my, look at the time. I must be going if I'm going to get to court on time." She began picking up the lunch trash and folding the blanket.

They drove down Benton Avenue past Stone Chapel on the Drury campus. It brought back memories of her four years she spent there. The campus consisted of three large dormitories, a library, athletic building, science building, business school, and outdoor track and field. It was one of the best liberal arts colleges in the nation. Off campus were a number of fraternity and sorority houses as well. Rooney continued to be an active alumna for the college and her sorority.

Just a few blocks from Stone Chapel, they arrived back at the shelter. She pulled up to the front door and let Michael out.

"Thanks for the ride and the conversation. I enjoyed having lunch with you and hope to see you again very soon," he said with a wave of his hand as he turned and entered the building.

Me, too! she thought. *Me, too.*

She headed back to her office. When she entered the building, she saw a policeman standing in front of the reception window. As she walked past the officer, he said "Ms. Rooney, could I have a moment of your time?"

"Sure," she said as she escorted him to her office and offered him a chair. "What's up? How can I help you?"

"I'm Officer Knight and I need some information. Judge Hal Sandrotas was kidnapped this morning from the parking lot behind the courthouse around eight o'clock. Since you're frequently in his court, do you know of anyone who might have threatened the judge?"

"You've got to be joking! Kidnapping a judge in Springfield? That kind of stuff doesn't happen here. What do you mean kidnapped?"

The policeman gave her the short version of the events earlier in the day. Her head was spinning as she tried to remember anyone who had threatened Judge Hal or was so angry in his court that they would hold a grudge. She couldn't think of anything that would merit that kind of revenge.

"I can't think of anyone who would want to harm him. At least, not off the top of my head."

"Well, if you think of something, just call the police station and ask for one of the detectives or Captain O'Malley. We don't have many leads at this point. Thanks for your time."

Rooney was stunned. *This kind of crime just doesn't happen here. Maybe they happen in Chicago or New York, but not here. I can't imagine what his wife and family are going through right now,* she thought. The remainder of the court schedule for the day had been cancelled. She had a few calls to make and some appointments to reschedule before heading to Ben's for a drink. What a roller-coaster ride the day had been!

Chapter Seven

In August, one month prior to Judge Hal Sandrotas's kidnapping, there was a private meeting of thirteen prominent citizens within the rectory of the Presbyterian Church of Plymouth, Massachusetts. Every community across the country has organizations and committees that hold meetings addressing concerns for the good of the public. However, there are secret committees or societies that address the personal concerns of their members. The most famous private organizations are the Freemasons, the Illuminati, and the Knights Templar. All are secret societies that have their own agenda.

Not all secret organizations have a mission for the public good. Some are concerned with more personal ambitions of their members, and others have an extreme approach to maintaining their definition of order in the community at large. There has existed for several centuries a secret society about which very little is known. This organization began after the landing of the Pilgrims at Plymouth, Massachusetts, in 1620.

William Bradford was the leader of the Puritans who left England in search of religious freedom across the Atlantic Ocean. As they established their community in the northeast wilderness, Mr. Bradford found the need for a council of elders to govern the people and to maintain order. This system functioned very well for over ten years. But as the population grew, they required a more formal judicial system to handle the increasing number of civil problems. The people elected judges and developed a court system to oversee disputes that arose among them. There was not always agreement that judicial decisions were just or that the decisions were in the best interest of the community. Therefore, the council of elders never disbanded and continued to operate privately to ensure that justice was served.

This group of elders became a secret organization. They would meet regularly and discuss the problems they saw that affected the Puritan society, be they religious, political, or agricultural. They were very effective in their role as guardian of the people of Plymouth. The Plymouth Council, as it was called, continued to operate as more and more English and Irish settlers migrated to the colonies. In 1653, William Bradford wrote a manuscript on the life of the Puritans during the early seventeenth century from 1620 to 1648. Included in the manuscript was a description of how they grew their food, how they dealt with the natives, and how they erected their buildings and their church. The explanation of their system of government was outlined in the document as well.

The manuscript remained in the possession of the Bradford family for nearly a century. Around 1736, it was given to Reverend Thomas Prince, who used it as a reference in his writings about the church and its members. After the reverend died, the manuscript was left in the tower of the Old South Meeting House in Boston. During the Revolutionary War, the British troops occupied the building, and the manuscript was lost for nearly a hundred years. In 1850, the manuscript was discovered in the Bishop of London's Library at Fulham Palace in England. Soon after its discovery, it was published. The original manuscript was returned to America in 1897 when Senator George Hoar of Massachusetts was able to secure its return. It now resides in the State Library of Massachusetts within the State House of Boston. However, all references to the council had been removed from the writings. It is thought that Bradford's nephew, who possessed the manuscript for many years after Bradford's death, was a member of the council. He most likely removed all references to the council to ensure that the functions of the organization and its members were kept secret.

The council was made up of thirteen members, a headmaster and twelve disciples. All matters brought to the council were discussed at length, and any recommended actions were then put to a vote by the disciples. In case of a tie, the headmaster would decide. Membership in the council was a lifetime commitment, and all were sworn to absolute secrecy for their own protection. As a matter of fact, no disciple knew the name, vocation, or city of origin of the other disciples. Only the headmaster and his secretary were aware of the backgrounds of the members.

To ensure the health of the council, all members were selected from the most prominent and wealthy citizens of the community. The council was well endowed financially. Upon the death of a member, the headmaster would select a replacement. Upon his death, the council would vote on a replacement from the disciples. The council has continued to function in this way for the past 350 years.

The headmaster took his seat at the head of the council table and opened the meeting.

"I call the council to order in the name of the Father, the Son, and the Holy Spirit. May God grant us the wisdom to proceed and resolve these matters He has brought to our attention.

"We are gathered here today to review a case involving a family law decision last year in a small town located in Southwest Missouri. One of our members learned of this case, and he felt it might require our attention. I have provided copies of the pertinent documents for you, and my secretary will hand them out for your perusal. But I shall summarize the facts for you now.

"The case involves the granting of parental rights of a small boy of six years old to his mother in a divorce action. It seems the father of the boy told the presiding judge that the mother was unfit to have sole parental rights due to a problem with alcohol. The judge in this case elected not to pursue an investigation in the matter. No friends or neighbors were called to testify regarding the charges made against her, nor was there any attempt to identify any alcohol-related illness or injury in the mother's history.

"Six months following the ruling in favor of the mother's right to sole custody of the child, both mother and child were involved in a motor vehicle accident in which the child died. The mother survived and was found to be intoxicated at the time of the accident. She was placed in an alcohol treatment facility for six weeks.

"Although the judge in this case, by law, could adjudicate the custody battle as he saw fit, it is my contention that due diligence was not given to the father's claim of alcoholism in the mother. If he had seen fit to investigate this claim, it is highly probable this tragedy could have been prevented and the child saved. There are others who have been involved with this case that will need our consideration as well. Should the council decide to proceed in this matter, I will seek your advice and recommendations concerning anyone else that should be included in this inquiry.

"Please review these documents. Take all the time you need. When you have completed your review, please close the file in front of you, and my secretary will retrieve all documents before we vote."

In less than an hour, all members had reviewed the case before them. The files were collected and locked inside a heavy wooden filing cabinet in the back of the rectory. The headmaster called the vote. It was unanimous in favor of intervening in this tragedy and evaluating if those involved were guilty of not protecting the child. After lengthy discussions, it was decided that those thought to be responsible for this tragedy would be detained and put on trial for failure to protect the young boy. Should they be found guilty of not fulfilling their responsibility to protect this child, they would be put to death by hanging.

"An eye for an eye and a tooth for a tooth, so say you all?" the headmaster asked as he stood up before the council.

And they all said, "Let it be so!"

The logistics of such an enterprise was not as difficult as it might seem. There were always people available to do their bidding for the right price. The headmaster already had a group of men he had used many times before. Within a few days, he had arranged for four men to complete this assignment: one as judge and prosecutor, two attorneys for the defendants, and one man acting as bailiff and jailer for the trial. He also hired a team of craftsmen to complete the erection of the courtroom, defendant cages, and the gallows. Of course, the greatest secrecy was demanded. Should they be discovered before accomplishing their task, there would be no final payment. None of the party hired for this mission was aware of the true nature of the council or its membership. Payment would be provided in cash, 50 percent up front and the remaining half after completion of the task. All communications with the team were made through calls from a payphone that could not be traced. The council had been down this road before, and all had worked smoothly with this group. As always, money was no object for the council, and they would pay the men well. Within three weeks, the call came to the headmaster that all was ready for the mission to begin.

"May God keep you safe as you do His work," he replied.

Chapter Eight

At 10:00 a.m. Thursday morning, Captain Richard O'Malley of the Springfield Police Department called a special meeting of all available patrol officers and detectives.

"I have called you all here to inform you of the development of an urgent situation at the courthouse. As you may have heard, Judge Hal Sandrotas has not appeared for court this morning, which was scheduled for about one hour ago. I received a call from Security Chief John Rose at the courthouse that surveillance cameras mounted around the courthouse showed he was abducted just after leaving his vehicle in the employee parking lot around 8:00 a.m. He was thrown into a panel truck and was driven off.

"We are launching a full-scale investigation for search and recovery of the judge. At present, we are at a loss as to why this has occurred, and we need everyone's attention to this matter. I have assigned Sergeant Greenwood to determine the minimum force he would need to cover the city for routine patrols and traffic management. For the rest of you, this is your only case until I tell you otherwise. The sergeant will assign some of you to specific locations to watch for the truck. I want you to talk to gas stations in the area to see if they've seen a truck like the one they used, which was a 1968 or '69 Chevy suburban panel truck. Check body shops that may have serviced or painted a late-model panel truck. Hopefully, if someone saw this vehicle, it will give us a lead to its escape route from the courthouse. I need each and every one of you to use your head on this investigation; keep your eyes and ears open. We know that in abduction cases, we have forty-eight hours to come up with a good lead or capture before things go downhill. So far, we haven't received a ransom call, but we can't wait for that.

"As you all know, Judge Sandrotas has been a great supporter of the Policemen's Fund. I need a happy ending to this case, and I need it quickly. Are we clear on what we face here? Are there any questions?"

"Do you have any other information about the abduction from the tapes, Captain?"

"It was a 1968 or 1969 Chevy suburban panel truck, either white or light blue. There were no external markings or signs on the vehicle. No plates were seen on the truck, but I will have Detectives Davenport and Hoover review the tape and verify that information for you. Are there any other questions?"

The room was in stunned silence.

"If not, you are dismissed, and I want you all back here at the end of your shift for an update. Until then, I want the patrolmen not assigned to routine patrol and traffic to canvass the courthouse and interview the court personnel and owners of surrounding businesses. Someone somewhere saw something we need to know about. So let's find it! If you hear of anything, call me here at the command post. Detectives Davenport and Hoover, give me a minute before you leave."

With that, the meeting was over, and everyone quickly filed out of the room. Captain O'Malley waited for everyone to leave before he sat down with the detectives. "Davenport, Hoover, this is your case. You have few clues to go on, but the best place to start is with his wife. They live in Southern Hills out by Lake Springfield. Start by interviewing her. After your visit with her, I want you to go over the tape of the abduction with Chief Rose at the security office in the courthouse. Maybe you'll see something that he didn't see. I talked with the chief just before this meeting and told him I don't want anyone to view the tape until he shows it to you. Got it? The city is looking to us to save this judge, and anything less than success here is unacceptable for them and for us. May God be with us all as we face this challenge, the likes of which we have never seen before in Springfield. Keep your eyes and ears open and protect yourself at all times."

Detective William Davenport looked at his watch and sat there for a minute trying to get his head around what he had just heard. Abducting a judge was a serious matter, and the usual reason was revenge. This could have a very bad outcome no matter what the investigation found. It's usually too late to save the victim, and he knew it. Not receiving a ransom call was not a good sign. Davenport was thirty-seven years old and had been on the force for the past fifteen years, working his way up from foot patrolman of the downtown area. He was over six feet of athletic muscle and unmarried except to his work. He was usually the guy that took the criminals down one way or another. Davenport was a product of Southwest Missouri State and loved hunting and fishing.

If he was not fighting crime, he was on the lake fighting bass and catfish. Davenport currently held the record bass caught at Table Rock, weighing twenty pounds, four ounces. He caught it two years ago, and it took him forty-five minutes to get it in the boat. His picture with the fish made all the regional newspapers, which caused a huge interest in Table Rock Lake for a long time. He mounted the huge bass on his office wall at home. He had a cabin down on Table Rock Lake, near the dam, where he fished mainly for bass. Below the dam, he fished for trout. About five miles from his cabin was a hunting club where he spent most of his free time in the fall and winter.

Table Rock Dam is relatively new and was completed across the White River in 1958. It supplies hydroelectric power to the southwestern corner of the state. The lake covers over forty-three thousand acres and has a shoreline of eight hundred miles, along most of which he had cast a fishing rod. They left all the trees on the lake bed, which many felt helped establish the fish populations that feed on the cedars and hardwoods. Table Rock is the place for catching bass, crappie, walleye, catfish, and spoonbill and for all water sports.

Five years ago, Davenport made detective and now had nearly a 100 percent conviction rate. He carries three guns at all times: a Smith & Wesson Model 10 Snub-nose .38 special, a Beretta Model 70, and a Browning Hi-Power 9mil. He sleeps with the Beretta. While he was patrolling Park Central Square about ten years ago, a bank robber ran out of the Missouri Bank & Mortgage building. He noticed Patrolman Davenport about fifty yards away and immediately pulled a revolver and pointed it at him. Davenport drew his weapon and fired, striking him in the chest. Although he lived, Davenport was given the nickname "Wild Bill" just like the legend of a hundred years before right on the same spot. Davenport filled his free time working with young men from his church. He coached summer baseball and winter basketball teams for twelve- and thirteen-year-olds.

Vern Hoover is his partner. Hoover is forty-five years old and moved from New York City, where he was a detective at the Tenth Precinct in downtown Manhattan. He married a Springfield girl and moved back west at her request two years ago. His wife graduated from the University of Missouri, majoring in business and finance. After graduation, she was hired by E. F. Hutton in New York City, a financial and investment firm. Vern met her while he was investigating a complaint of fraud within her company, which was later found not to be true. He asked her out on a date, and they were married a year later. They have two boys, one six years old and one eight. Vern is a lovable family guy who stands six feet four inches, weighs about 260 pounds, and is not what one would call fashionable. Actually, on most days, he is a little disheveled. Vern is a connoisseur of chocolate and he loves to try new and unusual chocolate treats whenever he can, which is daily. He will settle for any he can find. Of course, no one can make chocolate like New York City, as he frequently expressed to anyone willing to listen, which was not many.

Vern smokes too much, and Davenport tries to get him to quit. Hoover carries one gun, the standard issue Smith & Wesson revolver, which he has never fired. The thing that stood out most about Detective Hoover was that he had a terrific memory for details that most everyone else would have missed. He also brought a lot of experience in detective work from New York's finest. Aside from sifting through the clues, Vern felt his primary job was covering Davenport's back.

While in New York, Hoover had a distinguished career from 1958 until he moved to Springfield in 1968. He was the lead detective during the Bonanno Wars of the mid-sixties in Brooklyn and New York. The Bonanno crime family developed a split in their organization when the head of the family, Joe Bonanno, was felt to be spending too much time at his home in Tucson, Arizona, instead of Brooklyn. The split led to two factions, the Bonannos and the DiGregorios. In spite of efforts to reconcile and consolidate the groups, violence broke out in 1966 when a fierce gun battle erupted in a warehouse in Brooklyn. Thereafter, a number of murders and street violence ensued until Joe Bonanno retired in 1968 following a heart attack. Paul Sciacca became the new head of the family and tried with some success to unite the two factions again. From 1963 to 1968, Brooklyn was a very dangerous place. Hoover was credited with seven arrests for murder and extortion on both sides of the feud. He still misses the excitement of working mob crime in the Big Apple.

They both gave the captain their word they would not rest until they found the judge. Their first step on that road would be with the judge's wife. This was the hard part—having to deliver bad news. The judge and his wife lived south of the main part of the city near Lake Springfield. Davenport and Hoover's ride was a 1970 Oldsmobile 442. It was midnight blue with silver wheels and the meanest ride on the streets. It didn't take long for them to get anywhere, and within fifteen minutes, they arrived at the residence. Fortunately, it did not already have news crews crawling all over the front yard. They rang the doorbell of this quiet suburban home that would not be quiet for long.

Chapter Nine

The door opened, and Kathryn Sandrotas greeted them warmly. As they introduced themselves, they could see the blood drain from her face.

"Oh my God, what has happened?"

They took a seat in her living room and explained what had transpired at the courthouse. They had a few questions for her. Hoover quickly added that from what was seen on the tapes, there was no indication he was harmed in any way. Vern has a lot of experience in matters such as these and was able to put her as ease for the moment.

"Do you know of anyone who had a grudge against your husband?" Davenport began his questioning.

"My goodness, no. Never!" she replied.

"Have you or the judge ever received any angry phone calls?"

"Heavens, no!"

"Does he have any business partners other than those at the courthouse?"

"Only his accountant, and they've been friends for years. They go fishing together several times every summer down at the lake."

"Do you have any children?"

"Yes, we have two. We have a daughter who lives in Kansas City, and our son lives here in Springfield. Margaret works for the phone company there, and Thomas sells typewriters and word processors in his store on Glenstone Street near Sunshine. They adore their dad. I don't know how I'll tell them what has happened to him. You just have to find him! I can't imagine anyone hurting Hal unless ..."

"Unless what, Mrs. Sandrotas?"

"Unless someone from one of his court cases is taking revenge on him for one of his divorce rulings. People wouldn't do that, would they?"

Hoover looked her straight in the eye and said, "Whoever has done this, we will find them and bring Judge Hal home. There will be no stone we don't look under to find these people and bring them to justice. You have to believe that. The most you can do now is to get your family together. We will have an officer in Kansas City escort Margaret home later today. We will move all of you to a safe place for your protection until we know you and your children are not a target as well. You will have a police officer with you at all times until we are certain you and your family are not in any danger."

Before departing, the detectives waited for a patrolman to arrive who would take Mrs. Sandrotas to the safe house outside of town. As they left the house, it was becoming apparent that they would need to scour the hundreds of court cases to see if there was a link to solving this mystery. As they headed back to the courthouse, they radioed the captain that the interview with the wife yielded no significant information. Davenport called the security office at the courthouse from a pay phone at a gas station to let them know they were on their way. Hoover was busy making a list of things they would need in this investigation while at the same time buying a box of chocolate truffles from the candy store next to the gas station.

It was now almost 11:00, and the courthouse was still in lockdown. With the detective's approval, they cancelled the lockdown and allowed the court to resume some semblance of normalcy. The detectives and the security staff huddled in the small, cramped office to view the tape. The courthouse had recently installed a closed-circuit television system in the building. The system could monitor the outside of the building, including the parking lot and every courtroom. This new technology was spreading all over the country and could capture vital information if a crime or act of violence occurred on the premises.

Chief John Rose of the Courthouse Security Department was running the tape up to the moment of abduction for the detectives. Chief Rose had been a member of the SPD for several years before taking the position at the courthouse. He had developed some nerve damage in his left leg, which prevented him from doing the work as a patrolman and was offered this job a year ago. He was instrumental in getting the closed-circuit TV cameras installed, and this was the first case where it had been useful. As he was scanning the tape, Detective Hoover began explaining to the group what chocolate truffles were and how they were made when the chief pointed at the screen. "There, now watch this!"

Judge Sandrotas had just pulled into his parking spot when a light-colored panel truck approached. It stopped about twenty feet short of the judge's car. They could see him looking through his briefcase for a minute or two before he exited his vehicle. As he began walking toward the entrance at the back of the building, he passed the truck. Just as he did so, the double doors at the back of the vehicle opened, and a hooded suspect grabbed the judge and forced him into the truck. The vehicle slowly made its way out of the parking area, making sure they did not attract attention. The whole abduction took less than thirty seconds. After a few moments, Davenport broke the silence.

"Okay, we have a white or light blue 1969 Chevy suburban panel truck with no plates. There must be hundreds of those trucks in the area. Also, they've had several hours to exit the city and could be in Fort Smith, Arkansas, by now."

Chief Rose said, "As soon as I found this on the tapes, I called Captain O'Malley. He let his patrol officers know to be on the lookout for the truck. He has I-44 and Route 65 covered as well as Kearney Street out west and Division Street out east. They also plan to cover

Route 65 south, Sunshine out west, and Route 60 out east with the help of Greene County and Christian County Sheriff Departments."

Davenport was relieved to hear the major thoroughfares had been covered already. "Great! We're in the process of placing Judge Hal's family under protective custody and have officers at his home and in his office upstairs in case a ransom call comes in. We know there are at least two suspects in the truck, maybe more. Let's hope we get a lead on the truck or the hideout soon. All of our officers are scouring the area around the courthouse to find some information about the truck, which, thus far, is our only clue. Thanks for your help, Chief!"

With that, the detectives hustled out of the office. As they exited the building, a TV news reporter from KOLR Channel 10 approached them and asked for a comment. Davenport agreed.

"I am talking with Detective William Davenport of the SPD regarding the report of a daring kidnapping of a judge at the courthouse this morning. Detective, we have heard a judge was abducted from the courthouse earlier today. What can you tell us about it? Is it true?"

"Yes, unfortunately it's true. Our surveillance cameras recorded the kidnapping just before 8:00 this morning from the employee parking lot behind the courthouse."

"Which judge was taken?"

"Judge Hal Sandrotas."

"Do you have any evidence that he was injured?"

"No. From what we saw on the tapes, he was pushed into the back of a late-model Chevy suburban panel truck, light in color. So, if anyone out there watching this broadcast sees a vehicle of this type, call the Springfield Police Department immediately."

"Do you have any idea why this happened, Detective Davenport?"

"Not at this time, but we have identified several areas to begin our search, and we will update the public when we feel it is safe to do so."

"Thank you, Detective William Davenport, of the Springfield Police Department, who is heading this investigation of the kidnapping of family court Judge Hal Sandrotas. We will have a complete report on today's events during our newscast at 6:00 p.m. this evening. This is Bud Abbott reporting for KOLR Channel 10 News. Now, back to the station."

The search was just getting started for the truck. Davenport and Hoover returned to their offices to develop a game plan. They realized the only way to start moving the investigation forward was to find out as much as possible about the judge. They would have to interview his son and daughter as well as his personal staff at the courthouse. They agreed that the real answer to this puzzle must be in one of his court cases. Finding a definite lead pointing to a specific suspect from the court records would be about as likely as catching a marlin in Table Rock Lake.

Chapter Ten

That evening, the police department met at 6:00 p.m. to discuss their findings thus far and their plans going forward. All the patrols stationed around the city failed to find the truck used in the abduction. The visits to gas stations, convenience stores, and body shops all yielded no new information. The suspects had plenty of time to make their escape with Judge Hal before anyone knew he had been taken. The truck could be in a garage three blocks from the courthouse or hidden away in Arkansas by now. There were several trucks matching the one in the tapes found on the streets, but the drivers were local people with proper identification and registration.

The interviews with the courthouse personnel yielded nothing helpful. The detectives had assisted with the interviews both inside the courthouse and the surrounding neighborhood businesses. They planned to interview the personal staff of Judge Hal themselves. It was safe to assume that further surveillance of all major routes out of the city could be discontinued. That truck was well hidden by now in a garage or barn and probably would not be found in time. Captain O'Malley informed the group that regular patrols would resume in the morning as the detectives continued interviewing everyone connected to the case. The captain told the night crew of patrolmen to be alert for anything out of the ordinary. He asked everyone to be back for the morning report at 7:00 a.m., and they were dismissed.

Margaret Sandrotas arrived from Kansas City, accompanied by an undercover officer, after the meeting ended. She entered the precinct and was given a seat in Davenport's office. Davenport came in and introduced himself. He asked if she wanted some coffee, and she said yes, with cream and sugar. He provided her with all the information they had obtained about the kidnapping of her father, which wasn't much. A scruffy Vern Hoover entered the office wearing some of his supper on the front of his shirt and was cordially introduced. He offered his condolences for the terrible circumstances requiring their meeting. Davenport let her know that they would not rest until her father was returned to his family. He had a few questions.

"Ms. Sandrotas, do you know of any reason for someone to want to hurt your dad?"

"I haven't lived at home for two years, but I speak to them regularly. There has never been anything I have heard over the phone or during a few brief visits home that would indicate any problems. Everybody thinks the world of Dad."

"That's what we've heard all day. He was loved by all who knew him, for sure. Are you aware of any business dealings outside the court?"

"Well, I'm sure he invests some money with the help of his accountant, but I'm not aware of any other business interests. He has no rental property, either. If there was something recent he was involved in, I'm sure Mom would know."

"I spoke with your mother this morning, and she was not aware of any either. Our conversation was brief due to the emotional stress she was under, but I'll talk to her again later. I'm sorry to ask you this next question, but we need as much information as possible about your father's activities. Are you aware of any infidelity on the part of either of your parents in the past few years?"

"That's almost laughable. Certainly not!" she replied.

"That's all I have at the moment, but we do appreciate you coming back to Springfield so quickly. If I need any more information, I'll call you at the safe house. Detective Hoover, do you have any other questions for Ms. Sandrotas?"

"Yes, I do. Margaret, does your dad have a will?"

"What does that have to do with anything?"

"Actually, it may have a lot to do with this investigation if one exists," Vern stated in a matter-of-fact manner.

"Well, I think he does."

"Where does he keep it?"

"There's a copy in the safe at home, and his accountant has a copy. You're not asking me these questions because you think he's already dead, are you?"

"Not at all! The will could indicate some financial obligation to someone of interest to us in the investigation. Keep in mind we have very little to go on right now, and every little bit of information is helpful. How long have you been in Kansas City?"

"I moved there in 1968."

"Are you married?"

"No but I have a fiancé. His name is Luke O'Reilly."

"What does Luke do in Kansas City?"

"He's an accountant. We plan to get married next June here in Springfield."

"How long have you known Luke?"

"About three years."

"You both get along pretty well, do you?"

"Oh, yes. We have a great relationship. He and Dad get along quite well when they're together. I'm sure Luke has nothing to do with this."

"Are you older or younger than your brother Thomas?"

"I'm two years older."

"Did you go to college here in Springfield?"

"Yes, I attended Drury College and majored in business administration."

"What do you do for AT&T Telephone in KC?"

"I'm a marketing analyst for the company. I help to formulate plans for marketing new communication systems, primarily with small businesses."

"Has anyone asked you for a favor like giving them a system and not having to pay for it if they give you some money under the table?"

"No, that hasn't happened, and it would be difficult to accomplish because all systems are billed from the company headquarters before they're installed. It's not something I could give away without the company being involved. Also, I don't have access to the hardware that comes with the new systems."

"Thank you so much for your time and coming down to Springfield so quickly. You have been very helpful. We all pray for your father's safe return. We're also concerned for your safety as this plays out, and I know you want to be with your mother and brother. You will be informed of every detail we uncover. The officer standing outside the office will take you to the safe house to be with your family. I know you need to get back to Kansas City, and we're doing everything we can to bring this ordeal to a quick resolution."

Margaret slowly rose to her feet. "Please find my dad."

As she left, Davenport turned to Hoover and asked what he had on his mind about the will. "Well, these abductions are usually the result of two things—money or sex, usually both. The sooner we find the trail leading to one of these, the sooner we might get the judge back."

With that, Hoover pulled out a sack of chocolate covered caramels as he left the office. The detectives planned to head home with their police radios in hand and more questions than answers on their minds. They would return to the precinct at 7:00 a.m. for morning roll call unless something turned up overnight.

The police officer took Margaret to the safe house, where the family had a tearful reunion. The family was suffering, and everyone prayed for a quick and successful end to this ordeal. Still no ransom call had come in, and with each passing hour, the situation became more intense. Maybe tomorrow would bring them some leads.

Chapter Eleven

Rooney showed up at Gentle Ben's around 8:00 Thursday evening. The court schedule was in disarray from the events of the morning. All court cases were cancelled until Monday, September 21. That meant all cases had to be rescheduled, both at the courthouse as well as in the attorneys' offices. On top of the extra workload, they all had to deal with this terrible situation involving someone about whom they cared deeply. She just couldn't imagine in her wildest dreams that something like this could happen. But it did. The entire courthouse was in an uproar. It seemed like every direction she turned, someone stuck a microphone in her face and wanted a comment about the tragedy and how it was affecting her, personally. The Sandrotas family had been removed from their home and workplace before anyone knew what was happening. Word spread that they were in a safe house somewhere outside of town to protect them from harm and from the news media. It would be weeks before the courthouse returned to a normal schedule.

Gentle Ben's was packed with courthouse personnel needing to drown their sorrows as well as the concerned public trying to get some information about the investigation. The air was thick with the tension of the moment. Appropriately, Michael was playing only the blues that night; nothing but the blues.

"Rooney, how goes it?" shouted Ben from across the bar.

She sat down on the only vacant bar stool and just shook her head. "Not good. This whole day has been a mess, but it doesn't compare with what the family must be going through. Worst of all, the police have no leads yet on why this happened. I'm not very hungry, but I'll take a glass of Chablis."

"So tell me what happened over at the courthouse today. I've gotten bits and pieces from several people already."

Rooney took a sip from her wine, and after a long pause, she said, "This morning, I spent a couple of hours at the office and then went over to the Humane Society to tour the facility. It's really a cool place, and the people there do a terrific job. Michael is such a great guy. He showed me around, and I met some of his canine friends. Then we went to Washington Park, just north of the Drury campus, with a sack lunch for about an hour and talked while we watched the children play.

"Afterward, I returned to the office, where a police officer was waiting for me. He told me what had happened to the judge. Since I'm in his court frequently, he had some questions for me about anyone I may have seen that had threatened Judge Hal or if there had been any cases where fights broke out. There are always a few fights between family members, but I can't recall anybody that directly threatened the judge.

"When I got back to the courthouse, the lockdown had been lifted, and I met with his staff. They were so upset. Word is they have a tape of the abduction from the new closed-circuit television cameras mounted around the perimeter of the building. They grabbed him right in the courthouse parking lot as he got out of his car this morning around eight o'clock.

"I met with Detective Davenport from the SPD. He wanted to know if I have heard any threats toward the judge during court sessions, but, of course, I haven't. The police are just beginning their investigation and have no other leads. They're monitoring as many roads exiting the city as they can, in hopes of finding the truck used in the abduction. It was thought to be a 1969 Chevy suburban panel truck. All major exit roads from the city are being monitored by patrolmen with help from both the Greene County and Christian County Sheriff Departments."

"What a mess. Do they think this is a revenge thing? You know with every court ruling, there's a winner and a sore loser," said Ben.

"That's the most likely reason for a judge to go missing. There's always some tension in court. But even in court, most of the decisions are ones that both parties expect. However, someone gets a huge alimony award or loses custody of their child, anything can happen. I've had to dive under a table before when a fight broke out.

"Anyway, depending on the case load, they may have a new judge brought in to cover for Judge Hal. Either way, the next three weeks or so will be very trying on everyone. I just hope they haven't killed him already."

Patti Jo came into the bar looking for Rooney and found her talking to Ben. She came up behind her and gave her a friendly hug. "I heard about the happenings at the courthouse. It's all over the news. What's the story?"

Rooney gave her a brief summary of the day's events, and she started on her second glass of wine. "It is all such a mess, both in court and in the office."

After a couple of minutes, Ben broke the silence. "Guess who had a date with a local piano player?"

"You're kidding? Rooney, did you?"

"No, I didn't. At least I didn't think I did. Well, maybe I did. I was given a private tour of the shelter, and then we had lunch together. That's all!"

"Oh, girl, let's get a table. I want to hear every detail. Don't leave anything out. How exciting!"

They left the bar for an empty table in the back room as PJ gave Ben a wink. They sat at a table not far from the piano where all the events of the day would be detailed. Michael waved to them as they sat down. As usual, there was a crowd around the piano asking Michael to play their favorite blues tunes.

Rooney was definitely interested in the mystery man, and the encouragement she was getting from PJ was tempting. Michael has such a kind, gentle, and unassuming personality, which made him so attractive. But, for now, she would just see how things turned out. They sat there listening to the music as Michael was playing songs from BB King's 'Blues is King' album. As she tried to relax in the back room of Ben's bar, Rooney became lost in her thoughts about the unusual day she had experienced. Little did she know, this day wasn't over.

It was close to 10:00 when Rooney said she had to be going. Tomorrow would be another busy day of rearranging schedules, and she had two new clients coming in for consultations starting at 9:00. She said good-bye to PJ and then walked over to Michael, thanking him again for the tour and lunch they had enjoyed earlier in the day. As she left, she noticed there was a line outside the bar waiting to get in. Ben had a goldmine there on South Street. An absolute goldmine!

Chapter Twelve

After roll call on Friday morning, the detectives headed over to the mayor's office in City Hall to give him a review of the investigation. Mayor Kevin Eaton was a politician but was also a really good guy. He had been an offensive lineman on the University of Missouri football team that won the 1962 Bluebonnet Bowl game against Georgia Tech down in Houston, Texas. He majored in civil engineering and after college took a job with the Springfield City Hall and sat on the police department's advisory board. Last year, he was elected mayor by a landslide, and word had it that he was eyeing the governorship of Missouri. At six-five, 270 pounds, nothing much stood in his way. The mayor and his wife, Janeen, were regulars at all the charity events held by the Policeman's Fund.

The mayor was pleased with the efforts of all those involved but was concerned that a ransom call had not been received. It made it look like the chances of recovery were slim indeed. He told the detectives to let him know if they needed anything; he wanted to help in any way he could. The entire resources of the city were at their disposal for as long as they needed them. The detectives outlined every bit of information they had and the results of the investigation up to that point with Mayor Eaton and his staff. There were a few questions but not many answers. After their meeting, the mayor asked them to accompany him for a press conference that had been set up jointly by all the television stations. They agreed.

The news conference was held outside City Hall, and all major news outlets were there. The questions centered on the television tape evidence and plans for the search. The actions taken by the police captain and the detective squad were outlined, after which the mayor informed the public that the judge's family had been taken to a safe house for their protection. The press conference lasted twenty minutes, after which the detectives went back to the courthouse to meet with Judge Hal's staff.

The building seemed like a morgue when they entered. There was little activity noted in the halls of justice since court was cancelled until next week. Only essential courthouse staff remained at work that day. When they entered the judge's chambers, they saw Officer James Barton, personal secretary Lolita Kyle, and court stenographer Jan Inman sitting patiently around the judge's desk.

"Mrs. Inman, why don't you get a cup of coffee and be back here in thirty minutes?" Davenport said as Hoover ushered Officer Barton into the courtroom for his interview. Davenport and Ms. Kyle remained in the office. When the others had left, Davenport and Lolita sat facing each other. She wore a brown and beige cotton dress that came to just above her knees. When she sat down, the dress pulled up to mid-thigh, revealing her long, shapely legs. Her dress had a plunging neckline, and she wore red lipstick. Her hair was blonde and fell over her shoulders down to the mid portion of her back. Though not truly provocative, her style was one that would attract most men, maybe even the judge.

"Ms. Kyle," he began when she interrupted his question with "No, please, call me Lolita."

"Sure. Now, Ms. Kyle, how long have you known Judge Sandrotas?"

"About three years. I've been his private secretary for the past six months."

"During that time, has anyone had an appointment with the judge that seemed angry or threatening?"

"I never heard anything like that in this office. The only people the judge meets in here are the attorneys and his staff."

"Do you find the judge friendly and personable with others?"

"Oh, my, yes!"

"Are you aware of any business dealings of the judge outside of court?"

"No, I've never heard him speak about any other business he's involved with other than the charity the police department has for underprivileged children. He's very active in that program and helps to promote the organization and solicits donations."

"Have you received any mail that contained money or checks for the judge?"

"No, we've never received any mail like that, and I open all the mail."

"Do you ever socialize with the judge outside of the courthouse?"

Lolita looked away and shifted in her chair before answering. "We have a Christmas party every year for the staff. Is that what you mean?"

"Well, not exactly." Davenport moved his chair a little closer to Lolita and said, "What I meant to say was do you and the judge ever party alone?"

Ms. Kyle had a momentary loss for words, and then she began to cry.

"I'm sorry to ask these questions, but I need to know. I have to know everything about Judge Hal if I'm going to piece together what happened and find him before he's harmed."

After a few minutes, Lolita collected her thoughts and composed herself. "Yes, I've been seeing the judge on a personal basis since I came to work as his secretary. I love that man, and I wouldn't want to hurt his family in any way. They would be devastated if this became known. You must not tell them. Please don't tell them!"

"I will keep our conversation here confidential unless I find that in some way your relationship with the judge has led to his abduction.

Do you know of anyone, anywhere that is aware of your relationship with the judge?"

"No, no! We have been very careful."

"Have you told any of your family members about you and the judge?"

"No, no one knows about us."

"Did you ever write a personal letter to the judge that someone could have read?"

"No, I never write anything personal to the judge."

"Did you ever party with the judge in public?"

"Never! We always met at my home."

Davenport sat there for a while as he pondered further questions. He decided he already had the most stunning information about Judge Hal's secret life with Lolita, and anything further would be of limited value. He would cut her loose.

"I have no further questions at this time. If you remember anything that might be helpful to us, here is my card with my phone number. Call me anytime day or night, and if I'm not there, the precinct dispatcher will let me know you called. Now, go take a break and get yourself together while I speak with Mrs. Inman."

Lolita got up, wiped the tears from her eyes, and slowly walked out of the office.

She's a fine looking woman! Wild Bill thought to himself.

The interview with Mrs. Inman followed, but she was clueless as to what happened outside of the courtroom. She would rarely meet with the judge for clarification of the court transcript but had little personal contact with him. She was married and was quite business-like in her manner, offering nothing useful to the investigation. Detective Hoover came back from his interview with Officer Barton. Likewise, the officer had profound respect for the judge and never witnessed anything out of the ordinary. He had, on several occasions, handcuffed a defendant in court who was found in contempt and sentenced to a few days in jail. He never truly saw a genuine threat to the judge during the past two years he had been assigned to his court. Hoover asked Davenport if he found out anything useful from the two women.

"Not much other than the judge and Lolita has been seeing each other secretly for the past six months."

"I told you sex would have something to do with it. Did she indicate that anyone may have found out about their relationship?"

"No. She felt quite certain that their activities have been kept secret from everyone, including his staff members."

"Then we have to pursue the money angle to find the connection between the judge and the suspects. I hope we find it soon."

"I hope so, too," Davenport added. "I truly hope so."

The detectives brought the staff together and informed them of the need to review the case records for the past two years from Judge Sandrotas's court. It was a daunting task, and they would need help from the personnel in the records department downstairs. It was estimated that between 350 and 400 records would need to be reviewed by Lolita, Mrs. Inman, Officer Barton, three record room employees, and the detectives. That would mean that each one would need to review about forty-five records. Davenport figured about twenty to twenty-four hours would be required to complete the review. The group headed down the marble staircase toward the records department.

When all were gathered there, Davenport explained the task before them and that he needed it completed within twenty-four hours, preferably less. He reminded them that all the information they reviewed was confidential, and if something was found, they should call the police station and ask the dispatcher to contact him. They had a couple of interviews to complete and would be back in a couple of hours to help them search the records. Everyone knew what was expected of them, and they dug right in. The detectives planned to talk to the accountant and the judge's son, who was at the safe house with his sister and mother. There was no time to waste.

3910. Post Office, Springfield, Mo.

Chapter Thirteen

The accountant was Mr. Mark Bannister. His office was a block from Park Central Square next to Rubenstein's clothing store. When they arrived, the secretary escorted them immediately into his office. Bannister was a heavyset man, in his mid-fifties, with thinning hair and a jovial face. He offered them a chair and expressed his concern about the missing judge.

"Judge Hal has been my friend for many years. He and I love to fish for trout down on Lake Taneycomo in Branson. We go several times each summer for a long weekend. I hope we get to do that again."

"We hope so as well, Mr. Bannister," Davenport began. "Our purpose in speaking with you is to determine if the judge had any business dealings with anyone outside of the courthouse. You know, like a part-owner in a business, rental property, something like that."

"I've been Hal's accountant since he was elected to the bench ten years ago. We met at the University of Missouri and have been friends ever since. He's a fine man. I can't imagine anyone wanting to harm him. Anyway, Judge Hal's business dealings are strictly limited to his job at the courthouse. Once, he and I thought about buying a cabin down on Gobbler's Mountain at Table Rock Lake. We thought we could rent it out to guys who go down to the lake for the bass fishing. Nothing ever came of that idea, though. We help him invest

76

his savings in some stocks and mutual funds, and we prepare his tax returns every year."

Hoover asked, "Is the judge a rich man?"

"No, sir, he is a middle-income guy, and his lifestyle is rather conservative."

"How much is he worth?"

"Well, that's confidential!"

"Okay. Is he worth less than $250,000?"

"It is considerably less than that figure."

"Does he keep a copy of his will here in your office?"

"Yes, I have a copy. Gentlemen, I know you have a need for this information, but if you would bring me a search warrant, I'll be happy to oblige. No one wants to help you more than I do, but I need the protection that the warrant will provide for my release of any financial documents of Hal's."

"Is his wife's name on the judge's account with you?"

"Yes, her name is on all of his financial papers."

"We will see her shortly and will ask her to sign a release of information form. Will that be okay?"

"Sure, that would be fine."

They got up to leave and thanked Mr. Bannister for his help. Davenport asked him to call if he thought of anything that might be useful to the investigation and gave him his card. He said he would certainly do that and then ushered them from the office.

Back in the car, Hoover said that he thought the accountant seemed very reliable and that the records he had on the judge would not be very helpful. If the judge was into something sinister, he wouldn't let his family or his accountant in on it. Davenport agreed. They would see what his son had to say about his father.

While headed to the safe house, they spotted a light-colored panel truck traveling at high speed on Route 66 toward Joplin, Missouri. Davenport placed his red, flashing police light on the dashboard and easily caught up with the vehicle, forcing the driver to pull off the road.

As he approached the truck, he noticed there were two teenagers in the front seat. He ordered them from the truck and asked them to have a seat on the grassy shoulder of the highway.

"Where are you two guys heading to so fast?"

"Nowhere, sir!"

"Well, in that case, you were going nowhere fast. I need your driver's license and registration."

"They're in the glove box."

Hoover opened the compartment and found the documents. The driver was nineteen years old and a student at Southwest Missouri State. Davenport reviewed the license and registration.

"Now, son, you were going 80 mph in a 50 mph zone headed away from town. Where were you going in such a hurry?"

"Nowhere, we were just messing around. Honest!"

Davenport thought for a moment and then said, "Well, let me go back to my vehicle and catch up on some paperwork while I wait for you two to decide to tell me what's going on here. No one is going anywhere until I have some answers, and they better be good ones. Okay?"

After about fifteen long minutes, the young men decided to reveal their plans with the detective. It seems they were on a beer run to Galena, Kansas, which was just across the state line west of Joplin, Missouri. Their fraternity refrigerator had run out of Coors beer, which was not sold east of the Kansas border. They were just in a hurry to restock the fridge. The story was believable, and the two young men didn't seem like felons or bright enough to abduct a judge. So he was going to let them go but not before he lectured them on the speed limit and reminded them that the drinking age in Missouri was twenty-one. He thought the young men understood his position quite well, and he suggested they return to campus without any beer. They were happy to oblige.

In ten minutes, they were at the safe house located about five miles west of the Springfield Regional Airport. Davenport always drove the 442. He refused to let Hoover drive when he was in the car with him because Davenport thought Hoover drove like he was from New York City, which he was. The farmhouse was a ranch-style structure of about 1,800 square feet. Behind the house was a large, detached garage that included the workshop of the owner, George Shepherd. George and Lucy Shepherd were retirees that had bought the farm about ten years before. George was a career Marine Corps officer who had been farming his two hundred acres since he retired. George and his wife were volunteers in the policemen's charity, where they met Davenport and Hoover.

The home was situated in the middle of the farm and could not be seen from Route 66 or from any other building or property. The city council had allotted money in their budget to place a closed-circuit television system around the house last year. The only entrance gate to the property was wired such that anyone entering the property would set off an alarm. It was quite a nice set-up. The Shepherds wouldn't take any money for their services boarding those in protective custody. As they approached the house, Officer Blatchford met them on the front lawn. So far there were no problems, and Mrs. Sandrotas had managed to settle down a bit. As they entered the home, they met Mr. and Mrs. Shepherd and thanked them for their kind and generous assistance in this case. They silently prayed that someone in Hal's family could shed some light on this mystery. Maybe Thomas was their guy.

Chapter Fourteen

Thomas came out of the front living room to meet the detectives. He resembled his father a great deal. He was about six feet tall and a little heavyset with thick, black hair and small, wire frame glasses. Everyone took a seat, and Mrs. Shepherd brought a tray of cups and a large coffee pot, setting them down on the table in front of the sofa. She told them to yell for her if they needed anything and then retreated back into the house.

Everyone took a cup of coffee and sat back into their chairs, waiting for Davenport to begin. "Let me bring you up to date with our investigation," he said taking a sip of the coffee.

This is really good coffee! he thought to himself. *It's not at all like the stuff they make at the police station.* He made a note to ask Mrs. Shepherd where she bought her coffee.

"Yesterday, we had posted every available officer on all the major exit routes from the city after Judge Hal was abducted. We had hoped to spot the truck driven by the suspects. Unfortunately, no one saw them. They had about ninety minutes to make their escape before we knew what had happened. Therefore, last night, Captain O'Malley withdrew the surveillance of the highways leading into and out of Springfield to reassign them to other duties. Detective Hoover and I have interviewed Judge Sandrotas's personal staff and Mr. Mark Bannister, his accountant. Although no concrete leads came from those interviews, it has provided us with some information for our data bank that may prove helpful in the future.

"His staff and the court records clerks are currently reviewing all of the judge's court records for the past two years in hopes of finding a clue as to why someone would want to hurt the judge. Have any of you remembered something since yesterday that you thought might be helpful?"

No one spoke up. As expected, they each had more questions than answers. So did the detectives. After a few minutes of silence, Davenport asked if the accommodations were acceptable. They all agreed that they were and expressed how much they appreciated what the Shepherds were doing for them. He then asked if he could speak with Thomas alone in the den. Davenport led him into the adjacent room, which had a large fireplace with a roaring fire. Davenport and Thomas sat on the leather couch facing the fire and sipped their coffee. "I have just a few questions for you, Thomas. First, let me tell you that everyone at the SPD thinks the world of your dad and we are dedicated to finding him and bringing him home safely. He has worked very hard for all of us in many ways and we view him as part of our family. We are all grieving with you on this case."

"I appreciate you saying that, Detective"

"Okay, let's begin. When did you leave home and get your apartment?"

"About eighteen months ago, and I moved over on Seminole Street across from the National Cemetery."

"I understand you have a store that sells typewriters."

"Yes. After I graduated from Southwest Missouri State, I opened my store on Glenstone Street behind the Village Inn Restaurant."

"Do you sell one brand, or do you have a variety of typewriters?"

"We sell all major brands like Royal, IBM, Smith-Corona, and Brother. But we also sell word processors, which are like typewriters but have a memory function that allows you to review and store documents. Then you hit a button, and the typewriter types the document perfectly."

"Isn't this new technology just amazing? It seems like every year they come out with something we can't live without even though we never had it before. Some things never change, and yet, some things change every day." Davenport stared into the fireplace for a few moments, deciding what questions he wanted to ask.

"How did you get started in your business? Do you have to purchase the equipment and then try to sell it or do you just have to pay a stocking fee and pay off the machine after it sells?"

"Actually, I have done both. Initially I accepted the equipment on assignment and paid a monthly stocking fee until it sold. But now I purchase the equipment wholesale up front. The interest in these machines for home use has really helped get the business rolling. Also, the Christmas season is coming up, so that helps as well."

"Did you have to get a loan from the bank to do that?"

"No, my dad gave me a loan this past January, which let me purchase my own equipment. But don't tell my mom. Dad said it was best to keep it between us."

"How much was the loan, if I may ask?"

"Fifty thousand dollars. I pay 2 percent annual interest on the balance with a balloon payment of the remaining balance in five years."

"So, your dad is like a silent partner in your business."

"Yeah, that's right."

"Thomas, do you recall your father ever getting into an argument with anyone about anything?"

"Not that I recall. But I'm not at home much anymore."

"Do you remember any strangers coming to the house?"

"No."

"Do you recall your father every going on a trip without your mother?"

"Several years ago, my aunt died out in Arizona, and Dad went out there for the funeral without Mom."

"How long was he gone?"

"Only about three days."

"Anything else you can remember that worried you about your dad?"

"Not at the moment, but if I think of something, I'll be sure to give you a call."

"Thomas, are you dating someone or engaged?"

"No, not at the moment."

"Have you dated someone recently and had a nasty break-up?"

"No, I have been so busy at work that I just haven't had the time or interest."

"To your knowledge, is there anyone upset with you either personally or related to your business that might take revenge on your family?"

"No, Detective, my life is pretty dull, and I have no skeletons in my closet."

"Thomas, thanks for your help. We will keep you and your family informed of every lead we uncover. Hopefully, you will be back in your homes within two or three days. Call me at the station if you think of anything that might be important to the investigation."

He gave Thomas his card, and they walked back into the living room with the others. Detective Hoover had produced a bag of Ghirardelli chocolates and was passing them around. Before he could begin a history lesson on Ghirardelli and California chocolate, Davenport told him they had to go.

"Oh, almost forgot. Before we go, I have this little piece of routine business in cases such as this one. Mrs. Sandrotas, could you please sign this release that allows us to review the judge's personal financial accounts with Mr. Bannister, as well as the information he keeps in his safe at home? We just want to make sure there are no irregularities in the way Mr. Bannister handles his financial business."

Davenport laid the form on the table, and she signed it without question. She then told Davenport where she kept a copy of the combination to the safe. They again promised the family they would keep them informed of all developments and that they would work tirelessly to find the judge. They thanked the Shepherds for their assistance and headed for the car.

"Oh, Mrs. Shepherd, where do you buy your coffee? It was really terrific!"

"It's called Columbian Dark Roast, and you can buy it at any Consumer's Grocery Store in town."

"Thanks, I'll pick up a bag."

As they headed down the road toward the entrance to the farm, Hoover asked about the interview with Thomas. Davenport grinned and said, "Oh, yeah! Unknown to the wife and the accountant, the judge gave Thomas a $50,000 business loan last January to purchase his stock of typewriters and to help fund his new business venture. So, how does a middle-income guy come up with $50,000 to give to his son that no one knows anything about?"

Hoover looked over and said, "It's always about sex or money! I think we need to follow the money and keep Lolita under surveillance. What do you think?"

"I'm with you! I'll drop you off at Bannister's office while I go by the Sandrotas's home and look through the documents in his safe. I would doubt the judge left something incriminating in his papers that could be seen by his wife or by his accountant. Then, I'll pick you up at Mr. Bannister's office within an hour and head back to the courthouse. Hopefully, something shows up soon."

Chapter Fifteen

The detectives drove back to the courthouse to assist in the records search. They had a sick feeling that the judge was deep into something that could very well cost him his life. It was beginning to look like the judge's problems could be personal and not judicial. He had covered his tracks well, but they now had a money trail to follow. It would be difficult to hide where the money came from unless he received it in cash.

Davenport and Hoover entered the courthouse and found their way to the records department in the basement. As they entered the spacious room, they found everyone swimming in a sea of stacked court records. They were all looking for the same thing—a clue, any clue. Davenport reminded them that they only needed records in which there existed fighting among the participants or direct threats to the judge. Hopefully, if this occurred, it was entered into the records, or else they would never find it. Also, anyone who was jailed for contempt should have their records pulled as well. He suggested they begin with court cases that were completed after October 1, 1969. That would mean they would initially concentrate on records that predated the loan to Thomas by three months.

They all continued their task in earnest. Davenport had arranged for someone to go by McDonald's to pick up lunch, and they settled in for the afternoon and evening. The records were rather lengthy, and this task would be burdensome and tiring. At 2:30 in the afternoon, a call came into the department for Davenport. He took the phone.

"This is Davenport. What's up?"

For several minutes, he listened intently to the captain on the other end of the line. His face became pale and distorted as if in great pain. He sat down slowly in a chair as he thanked the captain for the call. He stared at the phone for a while and then got up and looked at Hoover.

"Vern, we have got to go. We have another problem!" Then he addressed the staff that was waist-high in records. "I want you all to review only the court records that involved Judge Sandrotas and Attorney Rooney since October 1969. That should significantly reduce the number of records to review. You should be able to complete your review in just a few hours. If you find anything, call me! Once you have completed the records, you may lock up and head home. I'll call you if I need your help tomorrow." They all gave him their home phone numbers, and the detectives left the records department.

The detectives headed for the door. Once in the stairwell, Hoover asked, "What happened?"

"Attorney Lillian Rooney is missing!"

"You're kidding!"

"I wish I were, but this thing just got a whole lot worse."

Within a few minutes, they were back at the precinct and headed for Captain O'Malley's office. His face was ashen as he sat down and motioned for them to take a seat.

"I just got a call from a neighbor of Ms. Rooney who said her car was parked in the driveway and, apparently, had been running all night. They live in a community out east of town on Sunshine Street near Route 65. Also, Rooney hasn't been seen at her office.

"About 10:45 last evening, she saw Ms. Rooney pull into her driveway as a truck pulled up in front of her house. They arrived at the same time, and she figured she knew the driver of the truck. After she got out of her car, she approached the truck, which had a sign on it that said Southwest Plumbing. She figured Ms. Rooney was having trouble with her pipes.

"This morning, she went out for the newspaper, and Lillian's car was still in the driveway, which was very unusual. She approached the vehicle and heard the motor running. Thinking that Lillian had gone back into the house after pulling out of her garage, she thought nothing of it. Later, she was leaving her home and noticed the car still there in the driveway and the motor running. Ms. Rooney's briefcase was in the car and she knew something was very wrong. She said the truck looked like a late-model Chevy suburban panel truck, light blue in color. Because of what happened to Judge Sandrotas, she called our office. It looks like we have another abduction to deal with."

Davenport slapped his knee over and over again as he shouted, "I should have placed the family law attorneys under surveillance as well! We never thought they would also be a target, but we should have. My mistake, Chief! I should have expected the judge was not the only one involved."

It took a while for Wild Bill to calm down. He had talked to Lillian yesterday about Judge Hal's courtroom and found her very pleasant and quite attractive. He was impressed with her respect for the judge and her genuine concern for his family. This case had just become much more personal for him.

"We will have the family law attorneys notified that a police officer in an unmarked vehicle will be stationed outside their offices and will follow them throughout the day as well as being stationed outside their homes at night. Sorry, Captain, we should have covered those bases up front. This was my fault!"

"Don't beat yourself up over this. We've all been searching in the dark on this one from the start," the Captain said.

Hoover saw some advantage to these developments. "This gives us the direction we have not had up to now. First, it definitely involves a case in the judge's court. Second, these guys knew we had their truck on tape. So why would they risk bringing the truck back out to abduct

Ms. Rooney? Aside from their plans to have both of them all along, they would have planned their escape from the city in such a way as to minimize being spotted. They waited for her to come home. Who gets concerned about seeing a plumbing truck parked in a neighborhood for a few hours? Once they grab her, they head back out of town before they're seen. It only would make sense for them to have their hiding place out east or southeast of town so they could quickly leave the area undetected."

Davenport thought for a moment. "That sounds reasonable to me. Captain, I would suggest you notify the Greene County and Christian County Sheriff Departments to beef up their patrols in that direction." He stood up and walked over to the wall map and outlined an area extending down Route 65 south from Sunshine Street toward Ozark, Missouri, and then east from Ozark north of the Finley River over to Highway 125, back north to Route 60, and then back west on Route 60 to Route 65 southeast of Springfield. Davenport and Hoover both agreed that it was highly likely that the suspects were hiding in that area and the sheriff deputies should concentrate on all roads within that seventy-five square mile area.

The captain told the detectives his office would make contact with the sheriffs and they needed to head out to Rooney's place to speak with the neighbor and check out the car. He would have two crime scene technicians come out to dust for prints, but they all knew the car would be clean.

As they arrived at Rooney's home, the neighbor came out to meet them. She said she had not touched anything and had left the 1965 Ford Mustang running. Hoover carefully opened the passenger door, wearing protective gloves to avoid erasing any prints. He reached in and turned off the engine. The interior had the faint smell of the attorney's perfume. He silently prayed he would see her soon. He removed the briefcase stowed on the passenger floorboard and shut the door. Nothing appeared to be missing, and there were no signs of a struggle. They reviewed and verified all the information given to them by the captain. It was just a clean bait and snatch. They both hoped it would be the last one.

———

Later Friday afternoon, a man by the name of Clem Skiles called the precinct and said that he had seen some activity in a small abandoned house next to his property the previous evening. He got concerned when he saw a panel truck parked behind the house a few hours ago. After hearing about the judge on the news last night, he thought he should call it in.

Davenport received the call on his radio and hurried back to the station. When he arrived, the captain had already assembled a team to investigate the site with a search warrant already in hand. Three officers would accompany the detectives. They loaded their weapons and put on their protective vests while they reviewed a map of the location. They were pumped with adrenaline. What a break this would be if it was the hideout they were looking for.

It took twenty minutes to arrive at the scene, which was just south of Willard, Missouri, west of town. They established a perimeter while Davenport searched the light blue truck out back. This truck had Missouri plates on the back bumper. The truck was clean, so he rejoined the others. Davenport asked Hoover to cover the rear exit while the others went through the front door. With all the window shades pulled down, they could only hear the people talking inside, but knew the building was occupied. Davenport quietly walked up the front steps, and when the officers were in position, he knocked on the door.

"Who is it?" one of the men inside yelled.

"We are collecting for the Salvation Army. Would you like to give a donation?"

"Sure, why not?" he said.

As he opened the door, Davenport pointed the Beretta in the guy's face as the officers rushed into the room. They found two other men stuffing marijuana into small baggies on a large coffee table in the center of the room. While the officers held the suspects at gunpoint, Davenport searched the house and found one more suspect in the bathroom. He called the "all clear" to Hoover, who entered from the back door.

"You guys having a party?" he asked.

The suspects said nothing, but it was evident what was going on with the large pile of marijuana on the table. The men were making one-ounce bags with intent to distribute. Apparently, they had been using the house for a while because two kitchen cabinets were packed with potato chips, Ho-Hos, and Twinkies.

"You just can't have a pot party without snacks, can you? Mama ain't gonna be happy with you boys!" Davenport said as he handcuffed each one.

They were read their Miranda rights and shoved into the back of the officers' cars for a ride downtown. Davenport bagged all the evidence and threw it in the trunk of their car. "Vern, I was so hoping this would be the place."

"Yes, me too, partner." It was a long trip back to the station. They had hoped the search southwest of town would have yielded some useful information if not the suspects, and it was time they caught a break. No one had called from the records department at the courthouse, so the possibility for some useful information from the record search was fading fast.

Chapter Sixteen

Just when Davenport thought things couldn't get any worse, they did. A call came into the dispatcher that a body had been found at Lake Springfield. A young man called and said he was fishing along the bank and stumbled over the corpse. He phoned from a nearby home and said he would meet the officers when they arrived to show them the location.

Darkness was falling as two patrolmen along with Hoover and Davenport arrived at the scene and found the young man waving to them on the north side of the lake. The body was just thirty feet from the edge of the water and covered with underbrush. They set up a perimeter for the crime scene technicians who were on their way but had not yet arrived. Davenport started carefully removing the debris that had been placed over the body when suddenly, he jumped back.

Hoover thought he must have seen a snake the way he jumped away from the body. "No, it's not a snake. It doesn't have a head!"

"A head of what?" asked Vern.

"His head! They cut off his head!"

The detectives and officers just stared at each other. After the initial shock had passed, Davenport resumed a careful clearing of branches and leaves from over the corpse. "Oh, my God! They cut off his hands, too! They sure didn't want this guy identified. No dental information and no fingerprints. Did you ever see anything like this in New York City, Vern?"

"No, I can't say I ever did, but we did have a bunch of drowning victims wash up on the banks of the East River. Now, let me tell you, that's a pretty gruesome sight. Several of my associates worked decapitation cases on Long Island. It seemed to be a favorite dumping ground for organized crime victims. They would remove any means of identification, including the teeth and fingers so prints and dental scans could not be used to ID the bodies. They would even kill elderly people who lived alone so they could assume their identity and cash their social security checks. I'm sure there were hundreds of bodies buried at sea or in Long Island Sound that we never knew about. Some people are really the scum of the earth."

The body was dressed in a white shirt and striped tie, which was still clinging to what was left of his neck. There was a large amount of blood present, which seemed to indicate he was decapitated where they found the body. "I sure hope he was dead before they worked on him," Davenport lamented.

"Yeah, probably a mob hit," Hoover said as he examined the torso, finding no evidence of any other wounds. "I would guess he was shot in the head and then brought here for the butchering. They took what's left of the head and hands and probably threw them into a wood-chipper somewhere."

"Vern, you certainly have a way with words!"

"Yeah, it comes with the job. Bill, we need to drag the lake just to be sure they didn't toss them in there. If not, we may never identify this body."

The medical examiner arrived and began a brief evaluation at the scene. He disrobed the body and found no evidence of bullet or stab wounds. Core body temperature indicated he had been dead over twelve hours. The pooling of blood on the front side of the body indicated he had been killed somewhere else and had been transported to Lake Springfield while lying on his abdomen. After the clothing was cut off the victim, the ME searched for other physical evidence. There wasn't any he could see, but everything was bagged for transport to the morgue. Hoover noticed a scar on the man's left knee.

"Hey, is that an injury scar or a surgical scar?"

The medical examiner carefully looked at the old wound and was quite sure it was a surgical scar. This guy had received some type of operation, probably a torn ligament repair.

"Great. I'll contact Mrs. Sandrotas to see if her husband has a surgical scar on his knee. Let's just hope this is not the judge."

"We also need to have these patrolmen canvas the area to see if someone saw the vehicle that brought the body here," Davenport added.

The trip downtown was a quiet one until Hoover started a lecture on where in the world the best chocolate beans came from. He said the cacao trees of southern Africa grew the best beans. Actually, they weren't beans but seeds. "You see, the fruit of the cacao tree is a pod filled with a white, pasty material that the monkeys love. But inside this stuff are thirty or forty seeds. It's from these seeds that the cacao 'bean' is made by roasting the seeds. Now my favorite chocolate is sold by Godiva. I like the dark, rich flavor of their chocolate. Makes me want to stop right now and get some."

"Are you kidding me, after what we just saw? How can you think about eating anything for at least a week?"

"In New York City, we found bodies all the time. Now, not like the one we just saw but some that were in pretty rough shape."

"Down here, we never see this sort of thing. I'll bet you were glad to get away from up there."

"No, not really. I only moved here because my wife wanted to be closer to her family and my family is in Florida. Working in downtown Manhattan was quite an experience. I enjoyed being a detective there because we always had interesting cases. This case we're on now is a really interesting case to me. But this town is a little too easy going to give us much interesting work. Now, I'll tell you who has the most interesting jobs in New York City—the vice squad. Just before I moved here, they had this case involving a group of transvestite prostitutes that—"

"Wait right there, partner! Let's not go any further with that story. I'm already feeling sick!"

"Deal, but I have to get something to eat."

Before they returned to town, Davenport radioed the station and had the dispatcher contact Mrs. Sandrotas regarding any surgery the judge may have had on his knee. Within two minutes, she radioed back that the judge never had any surgery, which brought some measure of relief to the detectives. The investigation of this murder victim would have to wait for the time being.

Davenport asked the dispatcher to put the captain on the radio. After a few seconds, the booming voice of Captain O'Malley came over the radio. "This is the captain. What did you find?"

"Not much. The body had no ID and was missing both hands and his head. Vern thinks it was a mob hit the way they removed any possibility of identifying him. Have you got any news for us?"

"No, nothing has been found and no ransom calls. I spoke with the sheriff departments, and they haven't found the truck or where the hideout is located. They're interviewing people in the area to see if they have seen a truck like the one we're looking for, but they have yet to call to let me know if they found anything. Why don't you guys call it a night?"

"We're going to have supper and then check back in at the station before going home. Call me if you find anything helpful from the sheriffs."

"Will do!"

Davenport put the radio down and thought for a few minutes about what they should do next to get this investigation on the right track. Nothing came to mind.

"Okay, Vern, what are you in the mood for? I'm thinking Mexican."

"Mexican is good."

"I know just the place."

Chapter Seventeen

They stopped by the Mexican Villa restaurant on the way back to town for some tacos. After supper, Davenport dropped Hoover off at the station to get his car. Vern had a few errands to run and would return later in the evening. As Davenport entered the precinct, an officer told him he had a male visitor that wanted to talk with him about the case.

"Good, I hope he has a lead for me."

As he walked into his office, he reached out to shake his hand.

"I'm Detective William Davenport. How can I help you or, rather, how can you help me?"

"It's nice to meet you. My name is Michael David Porter. I've heard a lot about this kidnapping case, and I want to help find them."

"And just how are you proposing to help find them, may I ask? Are you a private investigator or a family member?"

"Neither. I work at the Humane Society during the day and play piano at Gentle Ben's Bar & Bistro on South Street in the evenings."

Davenport couldn't help but laugh. "And just how does a dog catcher and piano player help me find them when my police department and two county sheriff departments can't find them yet? And we will find them!"

"With all due respect, you will not find them in time. I believe they're still alive, but there's little time left for them. I think that I can find them because I have the best investigator in the world working for me."

"And who would that be, young man?"

"Blue."

"Who's Blue?"

"Blue is the best bloodhound in the whole country, maybe the whole world. Blue will find them."

"Now, I've heard stories of bloodhounds tracking suspects or victims in the woods, but this is a different matter. You see, these victims were grabbed and thrown in the back of a truck. Then this truck was driven somewhere God only knows and dumped in their hideout. No way your dog can track that, you hear me? No, way!"

Michael sat back in his chair and thought for a moment.

"So far, you have nothing on their location. All you have is hope that someone brings you a lead. You don't even have a clue which direction to search. You have interviewed many people, you have searched the streets for two days, you have followed leads that went nowhere, and, so far, you have nothing. In addition to that, I will bet you haven't slept since this nightmare began. What I'm offering is a possible solution."

"Michael, I appreciate your willingness to help find the judge and Ms. Rooney, but this is out of your league. It sounds like you truly believe you and your dog can find them, but you can't. Why don't you leave this search to seasoned investigators?"

"Blue is a seasoned investigator. Look at it this way; if Blue and I fail, you're no worse off than you are now. But if you refuse to let us help and they're found dead, you'll have to live with that. We all will have to live with that. What we can do for you will not interfere with your investigation. I'm not offering a lead in your case; I'm offering you the solution. If I'm right, you and your team will get all the credit. I only care about finding Rooney before it is too late, and it matters to me a great deal. Yes, I'm sure Blue can track Rooney even though she was driven away in a truck, wherever it is. The decision is up to you, but you need to give Blue the chance."

Davenport gave him a long look as he leaned back in his chair. "Look, I appreciate your offer to help, but I can't authorize you to join our investigation. However, what you do on your own is up to you. So if you and Blue want to do this, I can't stop you. Remember, these suspects are probably armed, they are certainly dangerous, and the police won't be there to protect you. What I will do is give you a police radio, and if you do find something, call me. Do we have a deal?"

"Deal! You won't regret this decision. Now, I need two things from you. I need the address of Lillian's home, and I need Patti Jo Dickinson's phone number."

"Why do you need that?"

"PJ will probably have a key to her house, and I need an article of Rooney's clothing to give her scent to Blue."

Davenport sat there with a puzzled look on his face for a minute.

"You really think a dog can track someone kidnapped and driven away inside a truck?"

"I'm sure of it!"

Davenport shook his head as he gave Michael the radio and the information. Michael thanked the detective for meeting with him as he turned and walked away.

Davenport just sat there in amazement. *Now I've heard everything. But if he finds them, I'm going to be the one with egg on my face,* he thought.

Michael called PJ late Friday evening and asked her to meet him at Rooney's house the next day. She agreed and said she could meet him on Saturday at 2:00.

"Michael, are you sure you know what you're doing? This could be very dangerous. How do you plan to find them?" she asked.

"I'll show you when I see you tomorrow. We will find her. I promise."

<hr />

Darkness had fallen, and the hideout was cold and foreboding in the dim light of a single lantern in the middle of the structure. The judge had been abducted thirty-six hours before, and Lillian arrived twenty hours ago after she was taken from her home. Nestled in a valley between rolling green pastures sat the old, rugged barn.

The barn had stood alone for the past two years since the adjacent house had burned down. There was no activity around the structure, and no cattle grazed the fields. It appeared quite deserted. About one hundred yards to the west was a ten-acre wooded area filled with oak, hickory, and elm trees. Inside the large double doors to the barn, which faced west, was another door. This door was made from the finest hardwoods available. There was no window in the door, which was four inches thick and mounted on ornate, heavy cast-iron hinges. On the inside of the door were two iron holders for a 4x6 wood plank to ensure anyone who could pick the lock still could not enter through the barricade. The other three sides of the barn were reinforced with 2x4s, and the barn could not be entered from the hay loft. It was filled with hay, and the stairs from the loft to the barn floor had been removed. There was no other entrance or exit.

The interior of the barn had been converted into a complete courtroom made from the very best Missouri hardwoods by master craftsmen. The judge's bench was complete with a leather high-back chair, gavel, and green Banker's light. The tables for counsel were crafted of fine deep, rich mahogany that matched the railings separating the main floor of the courtroom from the foyer. Behind the judge's bench was built a gallows for two. It was erected of pine and was elevated eight feet from the floor. Over two trap doors hung two hangman's ropes. Whoever built this place spared no expense. Lining the north and south walls were ten five-gallon gas cans, each filled to the brim. It appeared that whoever was going to use this courtroom didn't intend to leave any evidence behind.

In both corners of the barn's west wall were two iron cages. In the north cage sat a man in his fifties. He wore an orange prison jumpsuit, and his left wrist was chained to the wall of the barn. Inside the cage was a cot with a mattress, a small table, and a toilet. Likewise, the south cage was decorated the same, and a young woman sat alone on her cot. She was also shackled to the wall. All she could do was cry silently to herself. Neither Judge Sandrotas nor Lillian Rooney knew why they were there, but they did know it wasn't going to be good.

Just before dawn, a man entered the barn wearing a black suit and a clear plastic mask. The mask allowed you to see his face but the mask distorted his features, preventing anyone from recognizing him. He walked to each cage and gave his guests a sandwich and a carton of milk. As he left, he told them that court would be in session at 10:00 a.m.

Throughout the rest of the night, the only thing they could hear was an owl from the woods nearby. They both tried to guess what had brought them to this place. Thinking that they had done something so atrocious that someone would go to this much trouble to punish them only added to their feeling of hopelessness. There was little conversation between the two victims as they awaited their fate. It was a very long night as they sat there chained to the wall, fearing their court session.

Rooney began to think about all the plans she had made for her life after her law practice took off. She had shown very little interest in anything except that which involved her family law career. She had not dated anyone seriously, had no plans for a wedding or a family of her own, and had not been to church in several years. She had accomplished a lot for herself but had done little for others, and she felt so selfish when she looked back over her life. The only thing anyone could write in her obituary was that she was an attorney. Rooney had not volunteered her time or contributed even a small amount of money to any charity, and she felt so ashamed. Then she thought about Michael, who had given his whole life to helping others. She was so sad and heartbroken that she had not done more with her life.

God, help me! Please, help me, she thought to herself.

Chapter Eighteen

At 9:45 Saturday morning, the barn door opened, and in walked four masked men all dressed in dark suits, white shirts, and black ties. As they entered the courtroom through the railing gate, one man put on a judge's robe he pulled from his briefcase. Two men came into the courtroom, and each stood behind the counsel tables, where they opened their briefcases and laid a stack of papers on the table in front of them. On a nod from the bench, the fourth man opened the cages, and after freeing the judge and Rooney from their shackles, escorted them to the tables facing the judge. He chained them to the tables making sure the locks were secure.

The trial began with a statement from the presiding judge. "I am Judge Smith. I, and the three other gentlemen here, are employed by an organization dedicated to protecting the public from injustice. This organization is the unseen plaintiff in this case. It is their feeling that a severe injustice has been done by these two defendants. You may feel that these proceedings deny your constitutional rights. That may be true, but the victim in this case was denied his protection under the law.

"Mr. Sandrotas, your attorney is Mr. James, and Ms. Rooney, your attorney is Mr. Brown. I will now read your charges before this court. Mr. Sandrotas, you are charged with dereliction of your constitutional duty to protect and defend the rights of the citizens of Springfield, Missouri. These charges involve the child custody case of December

15, 1969, case number CC31-1876279. This case involved a dispute between Jennifer Logan and her estranged husband, Wilbur Logan, over the custody of their child, James.

"Court documents indicate you ruled in favor of the mother, Jennifer, to have full custody of James. However, Mr. Logan protested stating that she was unfit for custody due to a problem with alcohol. Although it was true that this complaint had not been brought to the court's attention during the divorce trial or the custody hearings, you elected to ignore the charge made by Mr. Logan against his estranged wife. Six months after the mother was awarded custody, she was involved in an alcohol-related traffic accident that killed the young boy. It is the feeling of this court that you failed in your duty to investigate this charge by the child's father and you failed in your duty to protect the child under these circumstances.

"Upon the completion of these proceedings, should you be found innocent of the charges, you will be released. However, if you are found guilty by a preponderance of the evidence, you will be executed, hanging by the neck until death. Do you understand these charges brought against you, Mr. Sandrotas?"

"I understand, but you have no right to judge me in this way. You must release us now! You will pay for this outrage!" he shouted.

Judge Smith calmly replied, "I will take that as a yes! Thank you, Mr. Sandrotas. You may be seated."

As Judge Smith focused on Ms. Rooney, she was helped to her feet by Mr. Brown. "Ms. Lillian Rooney, the court documents indicate you were the legal counsel for Jennifer Logan. In that capacity, you were involved in her personal life more than anyone. By my review of the records, you had known her for more than two years. Whether or not you witnessed excessive drinking on her part, I am amazed that during that period of time you were never concerned about her fitness as a mother. Also, at the very least, when confronted with the charge by her estranged husband, did you not ask Mrs. Logan if there was any truth to the charge? Why did you not offer the court a physical assessment by a physician to verify whether she did or did not have a problem with alcohol? I have no evidence that indicates you pursued this path to ensure she would be a fit mother to raise her child. Therefore, it is the position of this court that you have failed in your duty to protect this child.

"On the completion of these proceedings, should you be found innocent of the charges, you will be released. However, if you are found guilty by a preponderance of the evidence, you will be executed, hanging by the neck until death. Do you understand these charges?"

Amid the tears, she softly spoke. "Yes, I do."

Judge Smith continued, "Let me be clear. These are two separate but related matters. If one party is guilty, the other party may be found innocent. If one party is innocent, the other party may be found guilty. I suggest you spend the rest of this day planning your defense. You will now have two hours to confer with your attorney. At 9:00 a.m. tomorrow, Sunday, September 20, 1970, you will have an additional hour to discuss these matters with your attorney and to plan your defense before trial. I will serve as judge and prosecutor in these matters. Court is now dismissed and will convene for oral arguments promptly at 10:00 a.m. tomorrow morning. Court is adjourned!"

―――

Later that afternoon, PJ arrived at Rooney's place before Michael and waited inside. The empty house made this tragedy even more heartbreaking. She was already a nervous wreck, and now she would have to worry about Michael. Was there no end to this nightmare? It just kept getting worse by the day. Finally, there was a knock at the door.

When she opened it, she saw Michael and with him was the biggest dog she had ever seen. It had to weigh over a hundred pounds, and he looked like he had just been awakened from a long nap with long, droopy eyes.

"What have you got there, Michael?"

"PJ, I want you to meet Blue."

"Is he gentle?"

"He's very gentle. You can pet him."

As PJ bent down to pet him, Blue looked up at her and wagged his tail. His expression never changed, however.

"So, Michael, how do you propose to find Rooney and the judge?"

"I won't; Blue will! Blue is a bloodhound and the very best bloodhound in the entire world. His keen sense of smell is over three hundred times more powerful than humans. He can track a scent that is two or three weeks old. Since Lillian wears a fairly strong perfume called O de Lancôme, the scent should be easy for him to track."

"How do you know what perfume she wears?"

"My nose is pretty good, too. But not as good as Blue's nose."

"You really think Blue can track someone who was driven away in a truck? How can he find a scent of someone thrown into a truck and driven many miles away?"

"That's what's so amazing. God gave this dog such a miraculous sense of smell that Blue can find her no matter how she was transported from her home. The scent is always left behind if you can smell it. Blue can!"

"Okay, we shall see. What do you need from the house?" she asked.

"I need something Rooney would wear but not wash regularly, like a sweater."

"She does have a sweater jacket she wears in court when it's cold, and she wore it this week."

"Great! Bring me the sweater and put a few drops of the perfume inside and rub it in well."

After a few minutes, she brought him the sweater. He smelled the garment and looked up at PJ with a smile.

"This will be perfect," he said.

Michael took the sweater and placed it in front of Blue. He whispered into Blue's ear, and the dog began pushing his nose and long ears into the sweater. After a minute or so, Blue sat down and looked up at Michael as if to say, "It's time to hunt!"

"Michael, are you sure you know what you're doing? This could be very dangerous. Have you ever done anything like this before?"

"No, not really."

"Then what makes you think you can find her?"

"Because I have faith that Blue will find her."

"Well, I'm glad you do, but I don't want you to get hurt, and I'm sure Rooney would feel the same way."

"Wouldn't you do everything you could to help Rooney, even if there was some danger?"

"Yes, I probably would. I'm just so frightened that this is going to turn out badly for so many people, and I don't want you to get hurt," Patti Jo said with tears running down her face.

"I know. But we have one chance to find her, and Blue and I want to take the risk. How about you?"

"If you're going, then so am I!" she exclaimed as she tightened her jaw and wiped the tears from her eyes.

Michael put a long leash onto Blue's collar. They walked out to the street where Blue picked up the trail. As Blue headed east, Michael asked PJ to drive the truck he had borrowed and follow them. After a few blocks, it was evident they were heading out toward Route 65 bypass, which would allow the suspects to have the quickest escape from the city. He put Blue back in the truck, and they drove to the interchange of Sunshine and Route 65. Once there, Michael took Blue out of the truck and let him nose around. After dodging the traffic around the intersection, it didn't take long before he found the scent. It led up the entrance to Route 65 South toward Ozark, a small community south of Springfield. Once again, Blue hopped into the back of the truck, and they headed down Route 65.

Within a few miles, they came to the large highway interchange of Routes 65 and 60 on the southeast edge of town. Route 60 West went back to Springfield, so they bet that the suspects had to go either south on 65 or east on 60 away from the city. First, they let Blue out south of the interchange on Route 65, but after fifteen or twenty minutes, he could not locate the scent. Michael, Blue and Patti Jo headed east on Route 60 toward Rogersville. After a quarter mile, Blue and Michael began walking along the shoulder of the highway. Within five hundred yards, Blue got a hit. His demeanor changed, and he became very animated and almost began to run down the road pulling Michael behind. Hopefully, the suspects kept the victims close to the city because Route 60 East ran all across the southern part of the state. Every one-half mile or so, they would let Blue out to see if the scent was still present. Each time he found it, Blue would look at Michael and bark. It was like they actually communicated with each other.

Once they passed county road NN about four miles east on Route 60, Blue lost the scent. To make sure, Michael drove several miles further east and let Blue search for another mile and a half. Blue could not pick up the scent, and Michael was sure they needed to track along NN. First, they hunted NN north of Route 60 without any luck. As they turned south on NN, Blue found the scent within three hundred yards. The road was narrow and hadn't been repaved in decades, which meant this was probably not a road for escape. This was a road to a destination. Darkness had fallen, and Michael decided to stop and resume the search in the morning.

Old Blue got a handful of treats and hopped back into the truck. "Blue will easily find the scent in the morning. This farm road would not be a road someone would take to get far away from the city. It's more likely that this road leads to their hideout somewhere hidden in this large area of empty farmland. It would allow them the privacy they need to operate."

"I agree. Someone could easily get lost out here and not be seen. There aren't any streetlights out here, either. Since we may be close to finding the hideout, let's keep searching. I don't mind."

"Blue and I will be going alone from here. I'm sorry, but it will be even more dangerous the closer we get to the hideout. It's best I go alone. We'll have to wait until tomorrow so we can see the buildings and pastures in daylight. But I promise you that I will let you know when we find them!"

Tears began flow from Patti Jo's eyes. "This is so terrible, so unbelievable! I don't know what I'll do if you're too late."

"We won't be too late; you have to believe that Blue will find them in time."

"You promise you'll call me when you find them?"

"Yeah, I promise."

Chapter Nineteen

Earlier on Saturday morning, Hoover met with the manager of Missouri Bank & Mortgage, where Judge Sandrotas and his son, Thomas, did their banking. With a search warrant in hand, he asked the manager to open the financial files on both of them. Within an hour, they had found a copy of the deposit slip and check that Thomas had deposited last January. What was interesting though was that the check was written by the judge on an account at the Southwestern Bank of Springfield. There was no mention of any accounts with that bank either in the financial records at Mr. Bannister's office or in the judge's personal safe at his home.

Vern called Davenport and asked him to call Judge Evans to get a search warrant for the Southwestern Bank records on the judge. Within an hour, Davenport arrived with the search warrant, and the two of them met with the bank president, Mr. George Harding. Harding came from what the locals called "old money". He was born into a wealthy family that had made its fortune in the trucking and transport industry. The company was founded in 1918 during the Woodrow Wilson presidency and World War I. The government had entered the war the year before, and the family began transporting military goods and weapons for the war effort. The Harding Motor Transit Company began as a delivery service for the United States and grew rapidly in its first two years.

The business continued to prosper and almost had a monopoly on the trucking business the first ten years. It continued to be the leader in the transport industry. The company posted a net worth of over $50 million with net profits of $3 million a year. Mr. Harding's father was the current head of the company, but George was positioned to take over the company soon since his father was in poor health. Several members of the family had started financial companies of their own off the profits of the trucking business.

George Harding started Southwestern Bank of Springfield in this way and had fifteen branch offices in the southwestern part of the state. Springfield served as the headquarters for this enterprise, and it reported assets of over $200 million. He was admired by his employees and was a deacon in the New Dawn Presbyterian Church on Fremont Street.

Mr. Harding had been following the story of the abductions like everyone else in town and was happy to help in any way he could. After a cordial introduction to the detectives, they focused their search on the three months prior to Thomas's loan. They soon found a deposit into the judge's account from November of 1969 in the amount of $100,000. The deposit and subsequent check to Thomas were the only transactions in the account. The deposit into Judge Hal's account was a cashier's check drawn from the account of Mr. Albert Richardson.

Davenport asked Mr. Harding if he knew Mr. Richardson. "Of course, he has been our client for many years. This has been a tough year for him, however."

"In what way?" Hoover asked.

"Well, his daughter and grandson were in an auto accident this past summer, and his grandson, whom he adored, was killed."

Davenport looked up at Harding and then Hoover. "I remember that case. She went through a nasty divorce and custody hearing, which led to her being granted custody just a few months before the accident."

Hoover shook his head and whispered to Davenport. "This is the connection we've been looking for. I'll bet Richardson bribed the judge to give custody to his daughter so he wouldn't lose his grandson. The money was hidden from everyone by using a separate bank not listed in his financial records. Now it all makes sense. The suspects have been hired to eliminate Judge Sandrotas for his crime. Rooney must have been involved in the case as well, probably his daughter's attorney. If that's true, this vigilante group wants to eliminate anyone connected to this tragedy, and Richardson may also be a target."

They thanked Mr. Harding for his help as Davenport gave him his card and phone number. "Certainly, I'm happy to be of service to the police. Call me anytime if you feel I can help."

The detectives left the bank after placing a call to the captain's office about bringing Richardson in for questioning.

Mr. Harding returned to his office and sat in his large, leather executive chair behind an ornate hand-carved desk as a smile came across his face. He picked up the phone and dialed.

The voice at the other end of the line asked, "Are all the chickens in the hen house?"

"We have one dead and two in the roaster. We are on schedule, headmaster!"

The detectives now had the explanation as to why this happened but had no idea of where the captives were being kept. What they needed now was to interrogate Albert Richardson in hopes he would come clean with what he knew. They radioed the station to get the address of Richardson's residence. He lived on National Street across from St. John's Hospital.

They took the Olds 442 and headed south toward the hospital. As they approached the neighborhood, the police dispatcher called informing them a body had been found at the location to which they were headed. It was Mr. Albert Richardson.

"They're eliminating those related to the case. We haven't got much time left. We need a break, and we need it now!" Davenport said as he punched the steering wheel.

They arrived at the scene to find two patrol cars already there. The officers were looking inside a car parked in the driveway. As the detectives got out of their car, two more patrolmen drove up. All the flashing emergency lights were a chilling sight for the neighborhood as people began to gather around the property. The victim was sitting behind the steering wheel of his car and slumped over against the driver's window. Mr. Richardson was the owner of a lumber supply company west of town and was a prominent member of the community. He and his wife had three children, including Jennifer Logan. The tragedy for this family just got a whole lot worse.

The detectives opened the automobile, which had blood spatter across the front and driver's windows. As Hoover entered the backseat behind Richardson, he saw the entrance wound to his head just behind the right ear as if the shooter had been sitting behind the driver in the backseat. This indicated to the detectives that Mr. Richardson probably knew the gunman if he let him into his car. If so, they were eliminating all those who were wrapped up in this case. Dead men tell no tales.

The rest of the Richardson family arrived at the home, and the officers escorted them to the neighbors next door to prevent them from seeing what had happened to Albert. The wife had to be taken across the street to St. John's emergency room for sedation while his children were interviewed separately about the tragedy and who might have been behind it. Of course, they knew nothing about their father's activities, but they were certain that their former brother-in-law had something to do with it. After the interviews, Davenport thought it might be a good idea to take Wilbur Logan into protective custody. The detectives had experienced enough stress the past two days to last a lifetime. They excused themselves once the social service people arrived to help the family through the stress of this ordeal. Hoover and Davenport headed for the car.

"We have collected two bodies, one we may never identify, and the other killed just before we could interview him. The records search revealed nothing useful, and no one knows anything!" Davenport said as he stood there shaking his head.

"I don't have a good feeling about any of this," Hoover said as he got back into the car. "We got nothing, Wild Bill, absolutely nothing!"

Davenport just sat there behind the steering wheel for a few minutes lost in his thoughts. He hadn't felt this lost since his wife left him three years ago. There are always a few things in your life you can't control no matter how hard you try. This case was one of those things, and his marriage was impossible to control as well. He had first met his wife while he was in college at Southwest Missouri State. She was a beautiful lady who was quite athletic and played on the women's basketball team. Her major was business administration, and, after she graduated, she became the personnel manager for Silver Dollar City in Branson, Missouri. It is a theme park built around an 1880-style community that included arts, crafts, and thrill rides for the children. Marvel Cave was the central attraction to the park, but it also had its share of music and theatrical productions. Davenport made detective just after they were married, and everything was great for a while.

As time went by, she became resentful of the amount of time his job took away from her. She traveled to Branson every day to work, which took about forty-five minutes one way, and when she was home, she expected Bill to be there for her. But that was not the case, and it became less so as his responsibilities began to mount. She loved her job, and he loved his, but there was less and less love between them. There were rumors that she was seeing someone else in Branson, but he never found out if it was true. He tried to alter his schedule, but the job had its own requirements, and they never seemed to be able to compromise enough that they could be happy together.

Finally, after two years of marriage, she filed for divorce, and he couldn't bring himself to contest it. Within six months, all the legal processes were complete, and they went their separate ways. As he looked back on the situation, he realized he never could control any of the aspects of their difficulties that led to the separation, and he knew very well that it was not going to end as he had hoped. He had the same feeling now. To make matters worse, his ex-wife married a professional bass fisherman. Some guys have all the luck!

On the ride back to the station, they went over everything that had happened and all their interviews. Maybe they had missed something. Who could be the one person upset enough about the death of little James Logan to mastermind this scheme to kidnap and punish the judge and the attorney. Maybe it was Wilbur Logan. He certainly would be mad enough to go to these extremes. It could be a close relative of his that had witnessed the suffering he had gone through.

"Vern, we need to look into the Logan family and see if we can find any answers."

"I agree. When we get back to the station, let's see if we can find any skeletons in their closets."

For the next two hours, they searched for information on the Logan family. Wilbur Logan owned two Chinese take-out kitchens, one on south Campbell Street and one on west Walnut. He was not a wealthy man by any means. He had two brothers who were carpenters and worked for a home builder in Nixa, Missouri. His parents were employed at Lily Tulip Cup Corporation as hourly wage employees and were not wealthy enough to finance a crime such as the one they were up against. Nothing seemed to fit. For now, they would put the Logan family on the back burner. They were losing hope that Judge Hal and Ms. Rooney would be found in time.

Chapter Twenty

At 9:00 on Sunday morning, September 20th, the barn door opened, and the legal team, on behalf of the council, entered the court. No one had slept in the barn last night. How could they sleep when they couldn't help staring at the gallows? The bailiff brought the defendants from their cages and secured their shackles to the legs of the heavy tables. They had one hour to confer with their attorneys, but they knew the guilty verdicts were a foregone conclusion. They spoke with the attorneys, but they could supply no new evidence or an acceptable explanation of their actions.

Precisely at 10:00, Judge Smith announced, "The court of the council will come to order!" as he rapped the bench with his gavel. "Mr. James, please present your opening statement."

"Your Honor, I represent Mr. Sandrotas in these proceedings. After a thorough review of the court documents, it is evident that at no time during the divorce trial or the custody hearings was there any mention made of Jennifer Logan having a problem with alcohol. It was only after Mr. Logan lost custody of James that he made this claim. It was a claim that was not substantiated by anyone involved in this case. Mr. Logan could have requested through his counsel that a physical and emotional evaluation be done on his ex-wife long before the case was finalized. If he truly felt she was an alcoholic, it should have been formally addressed in court. But he elected not to do so.

It is, therefore, our opinion that Mr. Sandrotas is not responsible for this tragedy and should be released."

The judge began his questioning of the defendant and his counsel. "Mr. James, was there any evidence in the records that Jennifer Logan was emotionally unstable or had difficulty participating in the proceedings?"

"No, sir. She seemed to be in control throughout the hearings and the trial."

"I noted in the transcript that Mrs. Logan had to be excused several times from court to use the restroom. This occurred during both court appearances of November 3 and December 15, 1969. No one else in attendance needed to be excused for any reason. Mr. Sandrotas, did that not seem odd to you?"

"No, sir. It is a very stressful time for people when they are in court. I didn't think it foretold an alcohol problem."

"Could it be she was consuming alcohol during these breaks to help settle her nerves, so to speak? She could have smuggled a flask into court."

"It's possible, but I really didn't know what she was doing. I wouldn't think it proper to question the lady about what she was doing in the restroom, for heaven's sake!"

"Have you ever had anyone else require so many breaks during a court proceeding, Mr. Sandrotas?"

"Not that I recall."

"So you must agree that with this unusual behavior, coupled with the husband's charge of alcoholism, an investigation into her possible abuse problem would have been warranted."

"I felt I acted with prudence in the courtroom and that her personal difficulties were never evident to me. Therefore, I did not seek further investigation."

"Mr. Sandrotas, were you aware that Mrs. Logan had been seen in St. John's Emergency Room on three occasions during the two years after the divorce was filed in your court?"

"No, I had no knowledge of that."

"Well, sir, she was seen on three occasions for injuries that occurred in her own home. The first visit was for cutting her hand with a knife while preparing dinner. The second visit was for injuries she sustained after falling down stairs in her home. The last visit was for falling in her living room, breaking the coffee table and spraining her wrist. She seems to have a lot of injuries, don't you think?"

"Yes, that is unusual, but this information should have been brought to my attention much earlier than just after the child custody ruling. I can't be held responsible for something about which I had no knowledge!"

"Is it your statement for this court that you were never aware of any alcohol problems in Mrs. Logan's medical history? Is that your testimony?"

"Absolutely it is!"

Judge Smith quietly read through the documents in front of him. After a few minutes, he looked down and asked, "Mr. Sandrotas, have you ever taken a bribe?"

Hal's face turned pale as he began to stumble over his words. Once he regained his composure, he softly said, "No, sir."

"Do you know a man by the name of Albert Richardson?"

"Yes, he's the grandfather of the young boy killed in the accident."

"Do you have anything else to add to your defense?"

Knowing that his secret had been exposed, Judge Sandrotas slowly sat down as he said, "No, sir. I don't think anything further would be helpful."

"Let's proceed to Ms. Lillian Rooney. Mr. Brown, may I hear your opening statement on behalf of Ms. Rooney."

"Your Honor, Ms. Rooney was the legal counsel for Jennifer Logan for two years prior to the final ruling on December 15, 1969. At no time did she speak with her other than on the phone, in her office, or in court. She saw no abnormality in her behavior, nor did she ever smell alcohol on her person. If she had, Ms. Rooney would have requested the appropriate evaluations to identify if a problem existed and to ensure her compliance with treatment. The late charge by her husband was felt to be an attempt to subvert the court's ruling that had been rendered. We, therefore, contend that Ms. Rooney is not responsible for this tragedy and should be released."

Judge Smith had just one question for Lillian. "Ms. Rooney, tell me what went through your mind at the moment Mr. Logan made his angry charge against his ex-wife."

"I thought it was preposterous. I never had any reason to suspect Jennifer Logan was under the influence of alcohol or any other drug. She went through a very stressful ordeal, and I thought she handled the stress well and without any medication or alcohol. It has always been our mission to ensure that the children live with and are cared for by the best parent or guardian."

"It didn't happen this time, did it, Ms. Rooney?"

"Apparently not."

"Ms. Rooney, do you have anything further to add to your defense?"

"I don't think it would matter if I did. I think this whole charade is just so some 'council' can feel they have righted a wrong. People are never perfect, and that includes everyone in this godforsaken place. Do with us as you must, but do it quickly!"

Ms. Rooney sat down, wiping tears from her eyes. Mr. Sandrotas was silent with his face in his hands. The judge took a few moments before speaking. "I find your arguments compelling, and I am aware that no one can truly know what is in the hearts of those around us. We all assume the best in others until they prove to us it is not warranted.

"However, there are some lines in the sand we should never cross when we are dealing with the lives of others. I will review all the documents and your testimony before giving you my decision at

10:00 tomorrow morning, Monday, September 21, 1970. We stand adjourned!"

After the court session was completed, the defendants were taken back to their cages. Judge Hal sat silently on his cot with his head in his hands. He knew his terrible secret was no longer a secret. He also knew there was no chance of him escaping the gallows that hung there in full view from his cage. What was he thinking when he took the money from Richardson? He knew why he took it. No matter what ruling he gave in court, there was always someone mad and someone who wanted an appeal. It seemed there were very few cases that ended with everyone happy. He never got the respect he deserved and never was paid enough to endure the humiliation of an appellate court judge accepting to hear an appeal on one of his rulings. All those appellate judges got their positions as a favor, so what was wrong with him doing a favor for someone just once? The money he got was nowhere near what the system owed him for the years of heartache on the bench.

Judge Sandrotas sat there for hours thinking how unfair this was, but he knew deep down in his heart it was his fault alone for taking the money. None of this would have happened if he had been true to his family and his profession, both of which he stood to lose in addition to his life. He began to weep at his acceptance of what was to come. There was no one he could confide in except Lillian. He felt sure she would be set free, and he alone would have to pay the price. It took him awhile before he could speak.

"Lillian, I am so sorry for what I have done. Please forgive me," was all he said.

It would be a very long wait for them to learn their fate. No one knew where they were and there was precious little time left for someone to find them.

Chapter Twenty-One

Sunday came with overcast skies and a colder westerly wind. Michael wore a heavy jacket with gloves and a stocking cap pulled down over his ears. He brought a blanket for Blue. After parking the truck at the Empire Propane Company parking lot on the northwest corner of the intersection, they began their search on NN south from Route 60. They walked about three miles, past an old cemetery and on further to Mentor Road. At that point, the scent led them east on Mentor. The farms along Mentor road were approximately four hundred acres in size, and many of the fields had the early growth of soft red winter wheat. Winter wheat was harvested in the spring and was used primarily in baking products. It gave the fields a beautiful and peaceful appearance during the winter as the wheat swayed back and forth with the wind. There was little traffic seen on the search that morning, but there was an occasional truck loaded with bales of hay or livestock. Mostly, the roads were quiet.

About a mile east on Mentor Road, there were three farmhouses on the north side of the road. Behind each house, there was a barn and equipment shed that housed tractors, hay bailing machines, and flatbed trucks for hauling wheat and hay. Many of the farms contained herds of cattle, such as Black Angus and Herefords, which were raised for beef, and Guernsey and Holstein cattle raised for their milk.

After traveling two miles east on Mentor Road, they passed the first and second farmhouses. Just before reaching the third house was a narrow, dirt road leading to an open field toward the north. Blue followed the scent about one hundred yards up the path, and as they entered the open field beyond, Michael told Blue they would stop and observe the area before them for any activity. Situated in the middle of the pasture was an old barn that faced westward toward a ten-acre area of heavy woods. There was no activity around the barn and no livestock in the fields. It appeared deserted. The field beyond the end of the path had tire tracks embedded into the soil, indicating someone had driven out to the barn on several occasions. With no other structure in sight, it appeared that the old barn situated in the middle of the pasture was the hideout for which they were searching.

Michael stood there for a few minutes and gazed at the rolling green fields surrounding this magnificent one-hundred-year-old structure. It had a hay loft whose door was open and swaying in the gentle breeze. Michael looked down at Blue and asked, "Is this the place, old friend?"

Blue looked up at Michael. Then he shoved his nose against Michael's pocket which was filled with dog biscuits as if to say, "Yes! I need my reward now!"

"Blue, you have done a great job! A truly magnificent job! I don't think we should press our luck any further. Let's go home."

―――――

Patti Jo Dickinson had given the detectives the names of two men that Rooney had been dating the past six months. They both lived in Springfield. Chip Evans was a trainer and body builder at the YMCA Fitness Center next to the Cox Medical Center downtown. At 1:00 p.m., the fitness center opened, and shortly thereafter, the detectives entered the building. They were struck by the heavy, humid air inside the place. It felt like a sauna and was filled with men and women of all shapes and sizes. It was easy to pick out the trainers from the trainees. Chip was helping an older lady figure out how to use the weight machine when they approached. He had "Chip" sewn into his shirt pocket.

"This must be the guy," Vern said as he put away the rest of his package of Oreo cookies.

"Hey, my name is Detective Davenport, and this is Detective Hoover. We need a moment of your time."

"Sure, what's up?" Chip replied as he led them into his office.

Davenport and Hoover followed him into the office, which had a full wall of glass allowing a view of the entire exercise room. They all sat down, and Davenport began by asking, "How well do you know Lillian Rooney?"

"Not well enough. She's a real fox!"

"What do you mean?"

"I mean she's one beautiful girl!"

"I understand you and she have dated."

"We had a few dates over the past four or five months. Why are you asking me about her?"

"Ms. Rooney was abducted from her home Thursday night."

"I didn't have anything to do with it!"

"You don't seem very upset about it. Tell me the nature of your relationship with her."

"We've had a few dates, dinner, movie, a couple of parties with friends, but nothing serious. I was hoping it would continue because I really like her. But I think a professional guy is what she's interested in, not a YMCA trainer."

"Did it upset you things didn't go further?"

"Absolutely not! Believe me, my life is full of beautiful women," he said as Davenport looked out over the exercise room filled with old ladies and fat men.

"Where are they?"

"Well, they aren't here today. Today is Senior Day."

"Yeah, I can see that."

"Have you ever been over to Rooney's house?"

"Just to pick her up. I've never gone inside."

"So if I found your fingerprints inside her house or her car, you wouldn't have a good explanation for that, would you?"

"No, I guess not. But I've never been in her house or her car. No, sir!"

"Okay, that about raps it up for me. Hoover, you have anything you want to ask Chip?"

"Yes, I do. Mr. Evans, do you own a truck?"

"No, I drive a '57 Chevy Bel-Air."

"Do any of your friends drive or own a truck?"

"I have a buddy who drives a Ford pickup."

"That's all I had. Thanks for your help and call us at this number on my card if you think of something useful."

As they turned to leave, Chip asked, "Is she going to be all right?"

"Wish I could tell you that, but no one knows at this point. Have a good day and thanks for your time."

The detectives waded through the crowd of senior citizens until they found the front door. At this point, they had no reason to suspect Chip was involved. He seemed like a nice guy and, for the moment, was not a suspect.

The second guy was Trent Newport. He was the owner of an athletic goods store near Twin Oaks Country Club south of town. Within fifteen minutes, they were perusing the counters for the latest in baseball gloves and sports jerseys. Davenport saw Mr. Newport in the back and walked up to him. "You certainly have a nice store here, Mr. Newport. How long have you been at this location?"

"About two years," he said as he was folding St. Louis Cardinal jerseys for the front display case.

"My name is Detective Davenport with the Springfield PD. This is Detective Hoover. Mind if we ask you some questions?"

"Am I in some kind of trouble?"

"Oh, no, sir! We just want to know the nature of your relationship with Lillian Rooney, the family law attorney here in town."

"Sure, I know Rooney. She's quite a gal."

"Have you ever dated her?"

"Yes, several times over the past few months."

"Is there anything serious between you two?"

"Pardon me, but why are you asking me these questions?"

"Well, it seems Ms. Rooney has been kidnapped!"

"You're kidding. That lovely lady? No way!"

"I'm afraid so. You wouldn't know anything about that, would you, Mr. Newport?"

"I can't believe this. Who would want to hurt her, of all people? No, this is the first I've heard about it."

The guy looked genuinely concerned by the news and then became nauseated. He began to perspire as his face turned white as a ghost. He looked like he might pass out.

"Whoa, partner! Here, let me help you into this chair."

Davenport guided him down into the chair. "You okay, buddy? You're not having a heart attack, are you? Want me to call for an ambulance?"

"No, I'm okay. There are some Coca-Colas in the fridge back there. Could you get me one?"

Hoover went to the back room and came out with three Cokes and the rest of his Oreos. They all sat down and waited for Trent to regain his composure.

"Hey, I thought I had lost you a few minutes ago. You okay now?"

"I don't know what came over me. This has never happened to me before. I think the world of Rooney and can't imagine anyone wanting to hurt her. This is awful."

"Yeah, it really sucks!" Hoover chimed in.

Davenport waited until the color came back into his face and said, "I'm sorry to drop this on you, but we have few leads and are just looking for something to put us on the right track. Did Rooney ever tell you someone was upset with her or held a grudge toward her?"

"No, she never mentioned she felt threatened by anyone."

"Did she ever tell you she was getting some angry phone calls or calls in the middle of the night and hanging up?"

"She never told me anything was happening like that."

"Okay, thanks for your time. Are you going to be okay?"

"Yeah, I think so. Let me know if you find her."

"Don't worry. The whole town will know when we find her. Here's my card. Call me if you think of anything that might help."

As they left the store, they knew they were no closer to getting any leads in this case, and it was a painful feeling for everyone. Every time they drove back to the station, it seemed like it took longer and longer to get there.

Chapter Twenty-Two

Sundays were usually his day off to play basketball at the YMCA down on Jefferson Street. Instead, he was manning the phones and checking in with the sheriff departments of Greene and Christian Counties after their visit with Chip and Trent. Nothing had been seen and nothing had been heard about the victims. Davenport sat there lost in his own thoughts and began to lament his impotence in solving the case.

Davenport and Hoover spent some time reviewing the findings at the Richardson crime scene from yesterday. By the position of the body and the entrance wound on the back of his head, he must have known the assailant to let him into his car. It might be worthwhile to investigate Richardson's past in more depth. The crime scene guys had dusted for prints but found only prints from his family members.

Vern sat down hard in the chair across from Davenport as he popped some M&Ms into his mouth.

"Want some?" he said.

"No thanks. Do you like pancakes?"

"Love 'em. What do you have in mind?"

"Today is Pancake Day at the Village Inn restaurant. All you can eat for a $5 donation to the Kiwanis Club. It's a civic organization that helps needy families and supports organized sports for the kids. Let' go and I'll buy."

"You're on!"

The restaurant was filled with families enjoying the feast. There was a long line waiting to get in, but Davenport knew the guys running the event and they were ushered through in just a few minutes. After they filled up on pancakes, a call came through Davenport's police radio. A detective in Rolla, Missouri, called back after requests were made to a number of other jurisdictions about similar abduction cases. They had notified every police department between Springfield and Tulsa, Oklahoma, to the west, Columbia, Missouri, to the north, Little Rock, Arkansas, to the south and Cape Girardeau, Missouri, to the east. Davenport called him from a pay phone at a gas station next to the restaurant. The detective quickly came to the phone.

"This is Detective Summers. How can I help you?"

"I'm Detective Davenport from the Springfield PD returning your call about an abduction case. I understand you had one a few years ago. What can you tell me about it?"

"Sure. It occurred in the summer of 1967. A local minister was abducted right out of the church parking lot as he returned from lunch. It was three days before we had any leads in the case. It was determined that the pastor had two separate lives, one heavenly and one rather worldly, if you get my drift. Well, the pastor was tarred and feathered, like they did in the old days. He escaped, and while he was being pursued by one of the captors, a local policeman saw them running across a baseball diamond. Apparently, it was quite a sight. He gave chase and captured both the pastor and the suspect. He was charged with assault and kidnapping.

"Since the pastor was from Illinois and had been carried across state lines, the feds took the case and he got thirty years in federal prison. He never gave up any other people involved. Let me tell you, that pastor was a sight to see! I think he learned his lesson."

"Where is this guy now?"

"Well, he had some mental problems, and they put him in the United States Medical Center for Federal Prisons, right there in Springfield!"

"Really, right under our noses! What's his name?"

"James Patrick Carnahan."

"I think we need to talk to this guy. Thanks, Detective!"

"We're in luck! This guy is right here in Springfield." Davenport called the Medical Center to speak to the officer in charge to get permission to pay someone a visit. "Hopefully, this guy will give us a clue to the mastermind of these abductions. It seems their purpose is to punish people who have violated the public trust. It sure looks like a vigilante group."

Hoover made a list of items he wanted to discuss with Carnahan. Vern had a lot of experience with prison interviews at the Attica Prison in New York State. He would lead the interview.

They arrived at the front gate and checked in. They had their weapons locked in a secured area at the guard house and then were escorted to the main entrance of the massive facility. Within minutes, they were in Warden Shea's office.

"Welcome, gentlemen, to our facility. I understand you need to interview one of our guests."

"Yes, sir! James Patrick Carnahan."

"Tell me why you need to talk to him, if you don't mind."

Davenport laid out the recent history of the case. "We had a judge abducted last Thursday from the parking lot behind the courthouse downtown. It was a clean snatch and was caught on our surveillance tapes. There are similarities in Carnahan's case, and we're hoping he will give us some information."

"I doubt he'll tell you much. He never cooperated with the feds and has refused to give any names. Now that he's a long-term resident here, maybe he'll be more willing to talk. The guard outside my door will escort you through the system and into the interview room. Remember, stay behind the divider that runs across the table. Your interview will be tape recorded. Any questions?"

"No, sir. We're good."

The guard escorted them to the first phase of three levels of security. They were again searched and ushered through a heavy sliding metal door. Once through, they held their position until the door closed behind them. As they entered the hall in front of them, they could see a fully glass-encased central office filled with television screens showing every area in the facility where prisoners had access. At the end of the hall, they were searched again and led through another heavy metal door that was electronically locked behind them. They entered the last hallway leading to the interview room. Once inside, the door to the room was locked, and they took their seats at the long, heavy table in the center of the room.

To their right was a large one-way mirrored glass, and in the right upper corner of the room was a surveillance camera that would tape their interview. Davenport was a little shaky, but he held his own. Hoover seemed right at home and said he was hungry. The door opposite the detectives opened, and in walked a tall, lanky, white man about fifty years old. He was dressed in a bright orange prison suit and sandals. Carnahan walked to the table, but before he sat down, he inquired about the nature of their visit.

"What do you guys want?"

Davenport was glad to see he was accompanied by a huge prison guard, about six foot six, three hundred pounds, standing just behind the guy.

Hoover answered, "We just need some information, nothing painful."

"Okay, what's in it for me?"

Hoover introduced himself and Davenport. "Depends on how helpful you are," Vern said, looking nonchalant and checking his watch. "Sit down for a few minutes and let's just chat. By my count, you have at least twenty-seven more years in this establishment or in one not as nice as this place. You give me information that helps me, and I'll make sure your parole board gets a nice letter about how you helped us out, confidentially, of course. It may cut some time off you current schedule. If you have pressing engagements on your calendar and can't speak with us, then we understand and are sorry to have wasted your valuable time."

Carnahan pulled out a chair and sat down. "You got a smoke?"

"Yes," Hoover said. He took out two cigarettes, lit one, and handed both to the guard who then gave them to Carnahan. He took a couple of long drags and then settled back into his chair.

"What's on your mind, detectives?"

"We had a very important member of our community abducted last Thursday from his place of employment. We thought of you with your experience in these matters and hoped you could shed some light on who is doing these jobs."

"Okay, ask away."

"Did someone hire you for the abduction of the pastor or did you do that one yourself?"

"I was hired."

"How many people were on your team?"

"Three."

"How many jobs have you done for these people that hired you?"

"Five or six, I'm not really sure."

"Did you know the reason you were asked to abduct these people?"

"Oh, yeah, we all knew."

"How did you select the victims?"

"We didn't. The main guy gets a call with the request for assistance. He then sets up the plan, hires the guys needed, gets the supplies, you know the drill. We never knew the people behind it all. The calls were anonymous."

"Who was the main guy?"

"Mr. Smith. It was always a 'Mr. Smith'. Never saw him before nor seen him since. These guys are very concerned about anyone finding out their identity and they don't like questions about who they are. I chose to leave it alone, if you get my drift, Detective Hoover."

"What type of people do you abduct?"

"They're all well known in their towns, important people like preachers, judges, school board members, city council people, you know."

"Did you kill any of them?"

"I wouldn't tell you if I had, but no, I had other responsibilities."

"What were your responsibilities?"

"I would build the hideouts."

"What do you mean, exactly?"

"You're not going to believe this but each of those jobs was for me to build a courtroom, a courtroom just like in *Perry Mason* on TV. And I don't mean just any old courtroom. I built them with better wood and materials than I saw in the federal court where they took me three years ago. This was top of the line. These guys have a lot of money, and they go all out for one of these jobs."

"Do you know where the calls come from, what city or state?"

"No, never. These guys are very secretive and have a lot of cash. That makes for a very dangerous combination, if you know what I mean. Therefore, you and I never had this conversation. Am I right on that, Detective?"

"Yes, I believe so."

"Anything else you can remember about the guys involved?"

"It would be painful for me to remember any of them, Detective."

"Davenport, do you have any questions for Mr. Carnahan?"

"Yeah, how much did you get paid for these jobs?"

"I got $25,000 up front and another $25,000 when the job was finished. It's all paid in cash. We got a call, and they would tell us where to pick it up. No delivery man brought us the money. We would just find it where they told us to look."

"Where did you hide your cash?"

"That's not part of our deal. Now, when do I get that letter for my parole board?"

"Soon, very soon. We do appreciate your assistance in this matter," Vern responded.

"Remember, this conversation never happened and never even speak my name outside this room. Got it?"

"Yeah, we got it. Have a nice day."

The guard led Carnahan back into the cell block. They sat there for a while and pondered the possible scenarios for the judge and Rooney. They now knew how and why, but they needed to know where—and fast. As they sat there, they began to think about how they would ever find the central organization of this enterprise. There was no national database for abductions they could review. They could search phone records, but the amount of data they would get from pay phones would be way too much for the small police force in Springfield to handle.

Davenport said, "The best bet for useful information would be credit card receipts and monthly account summaries from the suspects. Also, Albert Richardson owned a lumber supply company, and maybe he sold them the materials to build these courtrooms. Wouldn't that be ironic?"

"Well, there is never any love between thieves," Vern said, and he knew that well.

"We should also interview the owners of truck rental companies to see if we can get a lead on where the truck came from. Also, we need to check all local lumber companies regarding large orders of high-value hardwoods. We can begin that search after we get this case closed, and, hopefully, that will be soon."

They left the interview room and headed back through the maze to some fresh air.

Chapter Twenty-Three

As they returned to the station, their hopes of finding the victims on time were dwindling. They sat down in Davenport's office, feeling way beyond simple frustration, and turned on the TV while Wild Bill unloaded and cleaned his weapon. As luck would have it, on channel 10 there was a discussion going on between a news reporter and a concerned citizen about how disappointed he was that the police had not been able to find any leads in the mystery surrounding the abduction of a judge and an attorney.

"What are we paying all this money to the police department for if they can't do the job? It's just terrible!" the guy on the screen shouted.

Hoover looked at Davenport and shook his head. Just then, Davenport's radio squawked.

"Davenport, are you there? This is Michael. Come in, Detective Davenport. Come in. Over!"

Vern looked puzzled. "Who's Michael and why does he have a police radio?"

"Don't ask."

Davenport picked up his radio. "This is Davenport, go ahead."

"How has your day been, Detective?"

"Just peachy; so what can I do for you, Michael?"

"Nothing for me, but you can do something for the judge and Rooney, and you better do it soon."

"We're trying, Michael. What's up?"

"Blue found the hideout earlier today down near Ozark!"

There was thirty seconds of dead silence while the detectives wrapped their heads around what they had just heard.

"Repeat that, Michael!" Davenport said as his hands began to tremble.

"My dog Blue found where they're hiding the judge and Rooney!"

"Is this some kind of a joke?"

"No, this is for real."

"Where are you now?"

"I'm back at the shelter."

"Why didn't you call me on the phone?"

"Well, I never had the chance to use a real police radio before. When I was a kid, my dad helped me build a two-way radio, but it didn't work that well. But now I have a real police radio to use, so I chose the radio."

"And you're not putting me on?"

"No, it's the real deal. Why don't you guys come over, and I'll draw you a map."

"Stay put. We're on our way!"

On the short ride over to the Humane Society, Davenport gave Hoover the story of Michael and his offer to track Rooney and the judge down with his bloodhound. He couldn't formally include Michael in their investigation and never thought he would succeed in locating the victims. Loaning him a police radio was just a way to get him out of his office.

Vern appeared perplexed. "So this dog catcher and piano player tracked our victims driven out of the city in a truck and found our victims which we, you and me, the experienced and professional detectives, are clueless. Is that about right?"

"I couldn't have stated it better!"

They decided after they got the details from Michael they would plan their strategy back at the station while they called in the Task

Force. They sure hoped this was really happening. As they drove into the parking lot in front of the shelter, they saw Michael and Blue. Vern refused to get out of the car and said, "That's the biggest dog I have ever seen in my life! Holy smokes! You get out first!"

Davenport jumped out while Vern sat in the car waiting to see if the dog ate Davenport right there in the parking lot. He didn't, so Vern thought it safe to venture out. Davenport started by introducing Detective Hoover and then asked how he found them. As Michael reached down to give Blue a dog treat, he said, "I didn't. Blue did!"

"Okay, how did Blue track them down?"

"Well, Rooney wears this really strong perfume, which makes it much easier to track. Don't tell her I said that, though. She might be real sensitive about her perfume. That scent will linger for days, and even though you and I can't smell it, Blue can. He is just an amazing animal, isn't he?"

Michael outlined the directions to the hideout and described the old barn in the middle of a vacant pasture. He told them where the turnoff was to the pasture and then drew a diagram of the area around the barn.

Hoover was not yet convinced and asked, "Did you see anyone around the barn?

"No. We watched the place for a while, but I saw no one going in or coming out."

"So, you really don't know if this is the hideout, do you?"

"Well, there's one more thing. As we were leaving to come home, a light blue 1969 Chevy suburban panel truck with a Southwest Plumbing sign on its side passed us headed away from the barn. Yeah, I'm pretty sure!"

"Michael, I don't know what to say. If this pans out, I may want to hire you and Blue for our team! Thank you very much, and thank you, too, Blue!"

They returned to the precinct and began planning their approach to the barn. It was best that the assault be performed under cover of darkness so as not to alert anyone they were in the area. If they were seen before they secured the perimeter, the victims might be harmed. The Task Force had been recently developed for Springfield and Greene County, but it had never been used. The eight members of the Force were contacted and were told to meet at 6:00 p.m. at the SPD. That would give the team one hour for preparation before leaving for the hideout.

Davenport couldn't help but be amazed at what just transpired. He never gave Michael and Blue any chance of finding anything related to the case, much less find the victims. Somehow, Michael knew exactly what Blue could do in finding and tracking the scent. It truly was an amazing find, and, at that point, he couldn't be happier. He hoped they got there in time.

Chapter Twenty-Four

Night was falling when the Task Force assembled at the precinct. They were all excited about their first extraction of a victim by the team. The group was composed of the best officers the police force had produced. Three members of the team were detectives, four were patrolmen, and several of them had FBI training in Quantico, Virginia. They cleaned and loaded weapons, which included assault rifles and automatic handguns. In the tool chest, they had grenades, tear gas, a medical and surgical kit, special frequency task force radios, as well as gas-powdered portable saws for cutting through wood or metal.

The officers were dressed in black with stocking caps and face masks. It would be a chilling sight to see this team in action, and they were ready. They had reviewed the diagram provided by Michael and discussed their attack while en route to the hideout. The Task Force truck arrived on Mentor Road at 8:00 p.m. and parked about one hundred yards beyond the turnoff to the barn.

The team exited the truck and moved quietly down the dirt path toward the barn, veering off to the right to assemble in the woods west of the structure. The moon was nearly full and provided them enough light to maneuver over the uneven terrain. The extraction saw was brought along in case they had to open an exit path for the victims. Sergeant Eldridge was in charge of the team and reminded the men not to use their radios unless they came under fire. One officer was stationed at the turnoff from Mentor Road in case someone attempted to drive to the barn during the assault.

"We don't want to let them know we're here until we're ready to go in. Are there any questions?"

The group was silent. The sergeant called Officer Pinnell up front and asked him to survey the perimeter of the barn, looking for another entrance or exit other than the west barn door. He instructed him to find an opening in the wall where he could view the interior of the structure. Considering the age of the barn, there should be defects in the walls large enough to get a good look inside.

"Look for any movement inside and listen for anyone talking. See if you can determine the number of people in there. Be careful not to make any sound that would alert those inside that we're here."

With those instructions, Officer Pinnell advanced slowly toward the barn. For fifteen long minutes, they waited until he returned to the squad and informed the sergeant of what he had found.

"Sir, there are no other doors or windows other than the large west door. Through the cracks in the siding, I could see a single gas lantern in the middle of the barn sitting on a table. No one was talking, but I heard a woman weeping in the southwest corner. Also, there is a very heavy door erected behind the original barn door that blocks the entrance."

That was going to be a problem. In the event someone was inside guarding the victims, the only entrance was constructed such that a quick passage through the door was impossible. The sergeant met with the detectives to decide how to proceed.

"If we tip off the suspects too soon or it takes too long to break into the barn, it might give them time to harm the captives. We don't know what type of lock they have on that door or how difficult it would be to break through. What approach do you think we should follow? Should we break through a wall or try to go through the entrance door?" asked the sergeant.

Davenport was concerned that they did not know where the judge was located inside the barn and the door was probably barricaded from the inside. Breaking through the wall might injure the judge in the process or even knock the whole building down on top of them. There were several minutes of silence while they weighed their options. Hoover was sitting behind Davenport eating a Snickers bar.

Vern said, "You need a distraction!"

"What do you mean?" asked the sergeant.

"You have to draw them out. Let them open the door."

"And how do you suppose we do that?"

"Well, you could fire some tear gas grenades inside and force them out, but the distraction method would work better. You can bring that big truck down here and run it around the barn a couple of times with the headlights off. It has a pretty loud engine, but it's not threatening like someone ramming the door or using tear gas would be. Then, you park the truck behind the barn on the east side and let it idle. You wait for them to come out and see what's going on. There should be no sound other than the truck. Simple as that!" Then he downed the last piece of chocolate.

They thought about this for a minute or two and decided it might work. Davenport looked at Hoover and asked, "You've done this before in New York City, haven't you?"

"Yes, sir. It worked like a charm, too!"

"Then let's go with the truck distraction!" the sergeant decided.

The truck was brought slowly down the path. They turned off the engine and let it roll down silently in neutral. Once it was within thirty yards of the barn, the driver turned on the engine and made two loops around the barn and parked it on the east side opposite the entrance. The officer exited the truck, leaving the engine running, and took his station next to the back wall of the barn. The remaining officers had followed the truck and scattered around the building, with Davenport taking a position on the northwest corner and Hoover taking the southwest corner position that allowed them to see if someone came out the front door.

As the truck circled the barn, the lantern was extinguished. For five minutes, there was not a sound from inside the structure, and no one opened the door to the barn. They waited for what seemed like an hour as they debated in their minds whether this was the right approach.

The suspect, who had acted as the bailiff for the trial, had the job of guarding the victims, and he alone was in the barn with them. He didn't know what to do, but something was going to happen, and he didn't want to sit and wait for it without investigating his options. He elected to pursue a more proactive approach. He didn't care what happened to his prisoners, but he was not willing to take a bullet for them.

Finally, he elected to open the massive door. First, the large wooden beam was removed that had barred the door. Then he slowly turned the iron deadbolt lock and pulled the door open about two inches. He couldn't see anyone or any movement outside, so he opened the door just enough that he could slide out into the night air. He inched his way north along the west side of the barn toward Davenport and stopped before rounding the corner. His hands began to shake as he questioned what he should do. He decided just to peek around the corner to attempt to see the truck. Just one quick look was all he needed. As he turned the corner to scan the north side of the barn, he found himself staring down the barrel of Davenport's Browning 9mil.

"Lower your weapon and get down on your knees. Book him, Vern!" he said.

Hoover came up behind the bailiff and slowly removed the weapon from his hand, cuffed him, put him down on the ground, and sat on him. He checked him for other weapons and any ID. None were to be found. Davenport cautiously investigated the open door, but it was dark inside, and he couldn't see anything. He put his flashlight on the ground, pointing it toward the middle of the barn. He turned it on and quickly backed away in case someone in the barn decided to take a shot at him. Nothing happened, and all was quiet.

"Judge, Ms. Rooney, are you in there?" he yelled.

There were immediate shouts of laughter and crying at the same time. Davenport entered the structure and borrowed Hoover's lighter to light the lantern in the center of the barn. Using their flashlights, they stood in the middle of the barn, looking in amazement at the exquisite reproduction of the courtroom. He yelled to the team, "All clear!"

No shots were fired, and no other suspects were found. They released the judge and Ms. Rooney, who hugged Davenport's neck and wouldn't let go. "Oh, thank you. Thank you!" she said. "The others won't be back until 10:00 a.m. tomorrow for the sentencing phase of the trial. I don't know where they go, but they're always on time for court."

"Good. We'll have a welcoming party for them."

They surveyed the interior using police flashlights and were astounded at the quality of the workmanship put into this facility. The view of the gallows was a chilling reminder just how close the judge and Lillian came to being executed. They had called the Christian County Sheriff just before leaving Springfield to let him in on the takedown. He was observing the action from Mentor Road and quickly came down once they entered the barn.

Hoover gave the bailiff his Miranda rights and then shoved him into the back the sheriff's car. They had a cage just for him back at the precinct. They also placed handcuffs on the judge, who already suspected the word was out on his involvement in this crime. Rooney said she wanted to ride in the truck with the officers, and none of them had an objection.

As per protocol, the victims had to get a screening exam at the hospital emergency room before the briefing back at the station. They should have her home by midnight. As they left the farm and headed back to route NN, Rooney asked Davenport how he found her.

"I didn't; someone else did. I sure wish it had been me that figured out where you were. It would have been great for my career, but all's well that ends well!"

"So who found me?"

"It was Michael and Blue. Those two pulled you from the jaws of the Missouri Black Panther on this one, young lady!"

"You're kidding me! You've got to be kidding me!" For several minutes, she was speechless, and that was very rare for an attorney.

Chapter Twenty-Five

On the drive back to town, Lillian gave the officers a full account of her ordeal. The suspects were quite accomplished in the techniques of abduction and were very well financed. Since they always wore plastic masks, it was impossible to identify them. She and the judge were provided the bare essentials and were not harmed, except mentally. She described her capture from her home as the most terrifying moment in her life. The second most terrifying was the constant view of the gallows. Finally, she said the judge confessed his involvement with the Logan case and told her how sorry he was that she had been drawn into this nightmare he had caused.

"What do you think they'll do to him?" she asked Davenport.

"Twenty years in a minimum-security prison would be my guess."

"I feel so sorry for his family. He just threw his entire life and career down the toilet!"

"That about sums it up!" Davenport said as he shook his head. "You never really know people you associate with sometimes. Another part of this sad tale is that his son's business was built on bribe money loaned to him from his father. The feds will probably shut him down, or they might elect to just force him to repay the money. Who knows? Either way, they'll never get over it."

"Do you know who's behind this? This was a very smooth, well-funded operation backed by someone. Did you see that courtroom they built? It was nicer than our courtroom downtown!"

"Yeah, but in cases like these, you never know where the money came from. The guys at the top are so far removed from the operation that you can never identify them. That's what makes it so dangerous. The guys that ran this local operation are well paid, but they take all the risk. Tomorrow, we'll have the Task Force back in the barn waiting for the other suspects. Hopefully, we can get some information from them at that time. I expect they were contacted anonymously and paid in cash with no paper trail.

"Ms. Rooney, we'll get you checked out at St. John's ER and then get your statement at the station. It won't take long, and I should have you home by midnight. Is there someone I can call to stay with you tonight?"

"Yes, call Patti Jo Dickinson, and she'll meet me there. And please call Michael and let him know I am forever in his debt for what he and Blue did for me. Also, thank Mr. Hoover for his hard work as well."

"Oh, you mean the other guy, the guy from New York City," Davenport said with a grin. "Well, you'll see Hoover at the station, but you can tell Michael yourself right now."

"How can I do that?"

Davenport pulled out his police radio and handed it to Rooney. "Just push this button and speak into the transmitter."

She thought for a moment and clicked the button. "Michael, this is Rooney. Are you there?"

"I'm here!" he replied.

"The judge and I were just rescued and are heading back to the station after they check us out at the hospital. I just wanted to thank you for what you did, and I will always be grateful to you and to Blue. Maybe tomorrow sometime I can tell you in person."

"That would be swell! But thank the good Lord for this happy ending. He just used us and the people with you right now for this mission. You must have a special place in His heart to have been given a gift like this one."

"I can't disagree. Thanks so much, and I'll see you and Blue real soon."

The adrenaline rush of the past forty-eight hours began to subside. Rooney fell asleep as she leaned her head on Davenport's shoulder. They arrived at St. John's emergency room just after 10:00 and the check-up went well. The emergency room doctor did a quick physical exam and found she had suffered no physical injuries, but he feared she may have some post-traumatic anxiety about her captivity. Therefore, he gave her a prescription of a few Valium pills, just in case. Dr. Nabors was the only staff member in the ER that knew her true identity. Davenport didn't want the public to know of the rescue before they had taken the remaining suspects into custody.

Rooney called Patti Jo to let her know the good news, but she said Michael had already phoned. PJ was so emotional she could hardly speak. She would meet her at her house about midnight and would stop by the Brown Derby liquor store for a bottle of their finest wine, maybe two.

Back at the precinct, Rooney received a warm reception from Captain O'Malley and the entire police force, which had returned to the station to join in the celebration. Although the hour was late, all of those involved in the case wanted to be there when she arrived and to express to her how honored they were to be a part of her amazing story. They all knew that it took a very special and strong person to be able to handle such a terrible ordeal. She met with Detective Hoover and expressed her deep appreciation for his hard work and perseverance the past three days. After the party, she completed the police report and was ready to head home. Wild Bill escorted her to his car.

When she finally arrived at her house, she was greeted by PJ and her husband. It was a terrific homecoming. She hugged Davenport and thanked him again for his tireless efforts to save her.

"Don't thank me! Thank that dog catcher and Ole Blue for this one."

As Davenport left her home, he thought about what she and the judge went through and if he could have handled that situation as well as they did. To sit there in that dim light, chained to a wall in a cold and drafty barn while staring at your own hangman's noose had to be the worst experience one could go through.

The thought that someone could take it upon themselves to be judge, jury, and executioner of another person was unimaginable. This council had to be identified and put out of business, and Davenport was the right man for the job, along with Hoover.

The Task Force was informed they would meet at the station at 4:00 a.m. so they could arrive at the barn before dawn. This would prevent anyone from seeing the officers and warning the suspects of what was waiting for them. They only needed their automatic pistols and handcuffs for this one. Davenport had a few hours to rest before the final conclusion to this madness and decided to sleep at the station. At least he could rest a little easier. He let Hoover head home to be with his family for the next few days, now that the case would be closed soon. He hadn't seen much of his wife and kids lately and needed some time off. Davenport was so pumped he couldn't sleep, so he spent the next three hours planning a fishing trip. He decided he just might take Hoover.

Chapter Twenty-Six

The Task Force arrived at the barn before dawn as planned and parked the truck further down the road from the turnoff to the barn. They passed the time playing cards and talking about the case. Promptly at 10:00, they heard the panel truck arrive, which was then parked behind the barn. The suspects walked to the west side and knocked on the door, expecting their associate to open it for them. Davenport opened the door, and in walked the remaining conspirators wearing their plastic masks and dark suits. What they saw was nine automatic pistols pointed at their heads.

The takedown was uneventful, and no weapons were found on them. However, they did carry their driver's licenses with them. One of the men was from New Jersey, one was from California and, to the surprise of everyone, the third man was Mr. George Harding, President of the Southwestern Bank of Springfield. The interviews did not yield any useful information because the suspects had been contacted by phone by a group that wished to remain anonymous, and Harding had clammed up. It was obvious he was the middle man between the council and the operation there. The remaining half of their payment would not be forthcoming, so the detectives would not be able to apprehend the carrier of the funds. Mr. Harding was not providing any information. He knew the people he was working with, and giving them up was not an option should he wish to stay alive. They were taken to their own cages in the city jail.

It had been a long Sunday night as PJ and Rooney discussed the events of the past few days. Amid the tears, the laughs, and the wine, they came to realize that there was more to life than just thinking of one's self and work. Rooney made a vow to give more back, like volunteer at the animal shelter and participate in the Policeman's Fund for the children.

"This has taught me a huge lesson. I know that I'll look at everything in my life differently from now on."

And it deeply affected PJ as well. "Who would ever think that Michael David Porter and Blue would accomplish something like this? It just blows my mind!"

"You and me both, PJ. He's just a great guy, and I find him so fascinating. Maybe he'll ask me out on a date. What do you think about that?"

"I just want you to be happy, Rooney."

About 3:00 in the morning, they both fell asleep. At 11:00 a.m., the phone rang. Half asleep, Lillian answered the phone.

"Hey, you all up yet?" It was Davenport.

"We are now. What's up?"

"The rest of the criminals were taken into custody about an hour ago, and no one was injured. The only local was the Southwestern Bank of Springfield president, Mr. George Harding. Can you imagine that? Anyway, I've made it my life's goal to track down this council and terminate their operation, and that's a promise. The other reason for my call is to invite you both to a news conference and Welcome Home party at City Hall. The mayor has asked me to call and see if you could be at the courthouse at 1:00. He is going to make a public announcement about the successful efforts to free you and the judge. It's a combination of celebration and politics, if you know what I mean. But, it will be fun. Can you and PJ make it?"

"Well, I guess so. Yeah, we will! Thanks."

Rooney took a long awaited twenty-minute shower and got dressed. She decided to take the week off from work and to use the time to make plans for the new direction in her life. She had so many things that went on the back burner that she now felt she could tackle. She also felt the need to talk with Mr. Logan and apologize to him for not understanding the difficulties his wife was experiencing. It was just a terrible ordeal for all involved, and there were no winners this time. If she could survive this past week, nothing stood in her way. Besides that, it would be fun to get involved in more charity work, and even Ben might be interested as well.

Shortly after noon, PJ and Rooney hopped into the Mustang and roared down Sunshine Street, heading to the party.

They arrived at City Hall and parked in the rear to avoid the large crowd that had gathered in front along Boonville Avenue. As they entered the building, the guard escorted them to the mayor's office. Mayor Eaton and the detectives were waiting for their arrival. The mayor stood up and shook Rooney's hand, welcoming her back to freedom.

"I can't imagine what you went through and hope I never do. But let me state for the record that I have not witnessed anything that compares to this ordeal in my history as mayor or during my involvement with law enforcement. We are proud of you and your strength to get through this safely. It goes without saying, we have the best law enforcement team anywhere. Now, I would like for you to join me out on the front steps for my public announcement. Is everyone here that we want to be a part of this?"

Rooney looked at Davenport and asked, "Where's Michael? Where's Blue?"

"I called him this morning at the shelter and let him know about the festivities we had planned and told him when it would begin. He should be here by now. Maybe he's out on the front steps with the rest of the crowd. He did make it clear to me that he did not want any publicity about his involvement in this incredible story and that the real heroes were the men and women of the police and detective forces that made it possible. He's quite a guy!"

As they walked out of the building, a roar came from the large crowd awaiting the ceremony. There were news crews from KYTV Channel 3, KOLR Channel 10, KTXR and KICK radio. They all wanted to get a glimpse of Rooney and the detectives. The mayor stepped up to the podium and delivered a heartfelt speech about the quality of people that work for the citizens of Springfield, although some did not measure up to that standard. Judge Sandrotas and Bank President Harding were examples of how some people fail as public servants and as human beings.

"Thank you all for coming, and I present to you Ms. Lillian Rooney!"

The crowd cheered and clapped for several minutes before Rooney could begin. "I want to thank everyone who was a part of this operation for their courage and strength against terrible odds. I especially want to thank my friend and his bloodhound for their assistance because, without them, this wouldn't have been such a happy ending. To all my clients, I will be taking the week off to recuperate, and to all my opposing attorneys, beware! I'll be back next Monday." The crowd roared their approval.

After Rooney spoke, there were several local politicians that just couldn't let the opportunity pass without adding their comments to the festivities. From city council members to the school board, there was a train of people waiting for their turn at the microphone. Finally, the mayor stepped up and put an end to the speeches and again thanked everyone for coming out for the celebration.

"It truly is a great day for Springfield and our police force!" the mayor said as he turned and entered the building, taking the microphone with him to ensure no other speeches could be given.

As Rooney walked down the steps to the waiting news crews, she scanned the crowd for Michael. He was nowhere to be found. Everyone wanted to know how she was abducted and what she felt while living in an iron cage for three days. Of course, they asked about

Judge Sandrotas, but she said the case was under review and she could not comment on the judge's involvement.

As she began to leave, Ellen Clements from KYTV 3 News Department caught Rooney and asked for an interview. She agreed.

"Tell our viewers how it feels today compared to your feelings several nights ago when you were abducted."

"It's impossible to describe the feeling other than to say I was sure I was going to die, and now I have been given a new lease on life. I'm amazed how things have turned out."

"Were you harmed in any way?"

"Only emotionally. They gave us food and drinks, but otherwise we had only the bare necessities in the cages they locked us in."

"We were told they had built a gallows for you and the judge to be hanged. Is that true?"

"Yes, that's true. The gallows were right in front of us the whole time we were there."

"Did you get any information about who was behind this well-planned attack on both of you?"

"No, they never gave us any information about who was behind it."

"Do you have any comment for the Logan family?"

"I do, but I will speak to Mr. Logan in private."

"What are your thoughts about Judge Sandrotas and his family?"

"As you know, the judge will be arraigned tomorrow in court, and I can't comment on that case at this time. But I feel so sorry for what he has put his family through, and they are in my prayers."

"Thank you for talking with me on this exciting day for you and your family. I would like to interview you in depth about this case in a week or two when the dust has settled."

"I'll give that some thought, so call me in a few weeks."

"We are all grateful for your safe return home. This has been Ellen Clements of KYTV 3 News reporting with the hero of the day, Lillian Rooney. Now back to the station."

As Lillian and Patti Jo left, the Central High School marching band played as the attendees were treated to coffee and donuts. She felt humbled by the love shown her in the past sixteen hours. Rooney leaned over to PJ and said, "Let's go to the shelter to see Michael."

"Good idea!"

They arrived at the shelter around 3:00. As they walked into the reception area, Rooney was quickly recognized, and the few people there gave her their best wishes. Everyone wanted to shake her hand and to tell her how many prayers they had given up for her safe return. One elderly lady said she had never had a prayer answered so quickly. Finally they worked their way to the receptionist's window, and she asked if she could help them.

"Yes, we are here to see Michael."

"I'm sorry, Michael doesn't work here anymore. He left a few hours ago and said he had a new assignment somewhere else. I assumed it was with another shelter, but I didn't ask where. We were so saddened to hear he would be leaving because he's done such great work and everyone liked him, especially the animals. Can someone else help you?" she asked.

A pained expression came over Rooney's face. "How could he leave and not say good-bye? How could he leave and not let me thank him for what he did for me? Something's wrong. I just know it! He told me I would see him after I was rescued. He can't be gone!"

Rooney sat down because she thought she might faint. PJ bent down in front of her to try to soothe her emotions and to prevent anyone from trying to engage her in conversation. She held her hands and gave her a handkerchief to dry her eyes.

"It's okay, Rooney. It will be all right."

After a few minutes, Rooney got up and asked the receptionist, "Is Blue still here?"

"No, Blue was Michael's dog, and he left with him. I'm sorry," she said.

Rooney couldn't speak or move. PJ took the car keys from her hand and escorted her to the car. The ride home was silent. There were no words for this as Rooney quietly wept during the entire trip back to her home.

After entering the house, an exhausted and devastated Rooney sat on the couch and just stared at the blank TV set in front of her. PJ stayed with her because this might be another ordeal Rooney would need help in overcoming.

"This just can't be happening. Michael didn't seem like the kind of person just to leave and not say good-bye. We weren't close, but we experienced this nightmare together. I know he said his boss would call him about a job and he would have to respond, but not like this. Maybe something happened to him, and he didn't want us to know. Tell me what you think, PJ."

"I'm at a loss about this whole thing as well. But I'm sure there's a very good explanation and Michael will contact you. Maybe not today, but you'll hear from him very soon. Now get some sleep, and I'll stay with you."

Rooney dozed off to sleep for the next few hours. She was exhausted both physically and emotionally. All was quiet until 9:00 p.m. when the phone rang.

Chapter Twenty-Seven

It had been such a rough day for Rooney that PJ almost didn't answer the phone. Thinking better of it, she picked it up. A big smile came across her face as she gently shook Rooney, who was still asleep on the couch.

"Here, it's Michael!"

Rooney wiped her eyes, still moist from the flood of tears she shed throughout the day.

"Hello!"

"Rooney, this is Michael."

"Michael, I thought you left town."

"Well, I'm leaving soon, but I wanted to meet with you before I go. Could you meet me tomorrow at Washington Park?"

"Sure. What time?"

"How about noon?"

"Great, I'll see you there!" Rooney held the phone for a while and then looked up at PJ.

"It was Michael! He hasn't left yet."

"Yeah, I heard. I knew in the back of my mind he would call you."

"Oh, it will be hard to sleep tonight. What should I wear? What should I take with me?"

"I bet Michael only needs you there wearing anything you want, but don't forget your perfume."

"Don't worry, you'll never catch me without it. Why did you ask me to be sure to wear my perfume?"

"You'll see!"

The next morning, Rooney was up at dawn. She couldn't eat breakfast because she was so excited, but she did eat a strawberry Pop-Tart. The hours dragged by, which she filled with rearranging her closet, cleaning the dishes left from last week, and making a list of things she wanted to accomplish, starting next week. At ten o'clock, she showered, dressed, and made sure she didn't forget the perfume. She took the Mustang out of the garage and headed back to the courthouse to pick up some documents she was supposed to get last Friday.

She arrived at Washington Park shortly before noon. The children were there with mothers and fathers cautiously watching each one. The sun was warm, coming through a cloudless blue sky with a gentle breeze. She enjoyed the peace she felt there. At precisely noon, Michael walked up the street from the Drury College campus. He had a blanket, a basket of food, and, of course, Coca-Cola. He also had Blue by his side. The children ran to see the huge but gentle animal.

"Hello, Rooney! Glad to see you're looking well."

Rooney stood up, hugged him, and kissed him on the cheek.

"I don't know what to say to someone that saved my life. I don't know how to act around you, either."

"Rooney, you don't need to act. I think I know what you're feeling."

They sat down, and Michael opened the sack and took out cheeseburgers from McDonalds with two large Coca-Colas. While they ate lunch, Rooney gave him the play by play since she was abducted. When she had completed her story, she fell silent for a few minutes. "It was a life-changing experience for me."

"In what way?" he asked.

"I decided to volunteer at the shelter and to participate in the Policemen's Fund for children. I think there should be more to life than just ourselves and our jobs. I want to get back into my church, and I just want to make a difference. You know what I mean, Michael?"

"I know exactly what you mean, and I'm very happy for you and for the great work I know you'll do for others."

"So, tell me how you found me."

"Well, you have this perfume, which has a very unusual scent. It's a pleasant scent but one I knew Blue had never experienced. So, I suspected he wouldn't have any trouble tracking it. PJ and I got your sweater jacket and gave the perfume scent to Blue. With PJ's help, Blue tracked you to the barn. Once I was sure you were there, I called Davenport, and he arranged your rescue. It was your perfume that allowed Blue to find you."

As he was speaking, Blue came over to Rooney, wanting to lie down beside her. He placed his head in her lap. She stroked his thick coat, and the tears flowed.

"What happens now, Michael? Is there room in your life for me?"

"Of course there is, but not in the way you're imagining. You'll always be in my heart, but my job does not allow me to have conventional relationships. My boss has a job for me, and I must leave now to begin that work. But before I go, I just wanted to see you again and tell you how happy I am that things turned out the way they did. You're a lovely person, Rooney, and you have a giving heart with a lifetime ahead of you to do great work for the children. Also, I want you to have this."

He lifted a gold chain from around his neck that bore a gold cross. "My mother gave this to me when I was a small boy, and I want you to have it."

"No, I couldn't take something like that from you!"

"Rooney, I want you to have it. It would mean a lot to me to know you're wearing it. You see, my mother died last year, and I want you to wear it for me. Will you do that for me and Blue?"

"Okay, I guess if it means that much to you. Sure! I will always remember you and Blue when I look at it. Thanks!"

He draped it around her long neck, and the cross glimmered in the sunlight. It looked good on her; it really did. They sat there quietly and watched the children play. Several of the children came up and asked if they could pet Blue, and they wanted to know if he bites.

"No, Blue is very gentle and loves children. What's your name?" he asked.

"My name is Lucy, and this is my brother, Will. Over there is my daddy. His name is Mark."

"Hi, Lucy and Will. Who are your friends?"

"Her name is Karrington, and he is her brother, Kendrick. And that's Sara, Suzy, and their brother, Matt. He plays on a baseball team. Do you play baseball?" she asked.

"Well, not now, but I did when I was about your age."

The group sat down on the ground around Blue and began petting and talking to him. Michael looked at Blue and actually thought he saw Blue smile. They both seemed to be enjoying the action, and Michael had a huge smile on his face. Rooney noticed his pleasure at watching the kids.

"What are you thinking about, Michael?"

"I was just thinking about playing with my friends when I was young. The whole world is an amazing place to a child. I often think about my life when I was young and wish I could go back for a day or two. There was always something fun and exciting to do when you were a kid. Well, math wasn't much fun, but everything else was fun. You just never know how things are going to turn out. So, you just live for the day and don't worry about the next. It's too bad we can't be like children all of our lives. The innocence of a child is such a rare commodity in our world today. Children are quick to love and slow to anger. I can see why God loves them so. Rooney, do what you can to protect the children, both the ones you can see and the ones waiting to be born. God looks favorably on those who do."

Michael got a serious look on his face as he turned to Rooney. "I want to tell you something, Lillian. There is a lot of evil in this world, and people seem to blame God for all of it. They believe God either causes these things to happen or, at least, He allows these things to happen. God does not cause the evil things in our lives. He gave us the freedom to make mistakes, to take the wrong path in our lives, or to think only of ourselves instead of thinking about and loving others. Of course, He prefers that we would always choose the correct path, but He knew we would get ourselves into trouble and lose our way. True evil occurs because of the complete absence of God in our lives. He is a loving God, and even though we have difficult times, the process by which we heal and move forward in the right direction makes us stronger and wiser. You have been given a gift from God. Use that gift well in your life, and you can't imagine how many lives you will touch."

Michael got up and stood there for a while gazing at the children at play and the beautiful woman next to him who had gone through a terrible ordeal. He knew these events would make Rooney a stronger and more giving person, and it made him feel good.

"Well, I have got to be going, Rooney. You will always be in my thoughts, and someday we'll meet again. Enjoy your new life. Marry and have plenty of children. Get a dog for goodness sakes. But remember, you can't save them all. Just save the ones you can."

Rooney got up and hugged him as she wept. He held her and looked into her beautiful face. He smiled and then turned and walked away, leading Blue back toward Drury. She sat there lost in her thoughts for a while. She cried and laughed and watched the children play. She remained in Washington Park for over an hour, watching the children and just enjoying the day. She would deal with tomorrow when it arrived, but for now, she was just thankful for the amazing gift and wonderful friend she had been given. Finally, she got up and returned home. She didn't even call Patti Jo.

Chapter Twenty-Eight

A year passed, and things had returned to normal in Springfield except that Rooney had made good on her promise to support the Humane Society and several charities in the city. She had gotten over the events of the past and was still active in her law practice. It was booming since her abduction and rescue. Everyone wanted her for their attorney, the lady that defeated death. She saw the detectives now and again and had lunch a few times with Wild Bill Davenport. Life was good!

The day before Thanksgiving, 1971, she received a call from Patti Jo. "Rooney, have you been listening to KICK radio?"

"No, I've been pushing papers all afternoon, getting ready for the Thanksgiving weekend. What's up?"

"I was just listening to the radio, and the disc jockey introduced a new song that is just wonderful. Would you believe it's a song just released by Bill Withers called 'Ain't No Sunshine.' You know, the song Michael played and sang for you at Ben's place!"

"Oh, really. So what about it?"

"Don't you see? Michael played you a song that didn't exist! How would he know the exact words and music to a song that didn't even exist? In addition to that, he sang you a song about you being gone. Two days later, you were gone—really gone!"

Rooney had no answer, and it took a while before the significance of what Patti Jo was saying sank into her head. It didn't make sense.

"Okay, let me think about this, and I'll call you later."

She fell back into her chair stone-faced for several minutes. *How could Michael possibly have known about a song that hadn't been written or recorded?* she thought. It was late in the afternoon, and tomorrow was a holiday. She cleaned off her desk and headed for her car. As she headed home, Rooney remembered that Michael said his father was the owner of Gilbert's Gas Station on the corner of Grant Street and Division in midtown. Maybe he still worked there. She decided to pay Gilbert a visit. He would know where Michael was now living and working. It would be nice to speak with him again, as she had often thought about him and Blue.

She arrived at the gas station at 5:00 and pulled up to the gas pump. A middle-aged man came out to greet her. He had an uncanny resemblance to Michael.

"Hi, my name is Lillian, and, in addition to filling the tank, I need some information."

"Sure, let me fill it up, and you can wait for me in the office," he said with a big smile.

As she walked into the office, she noticed a Coca-Cola machine standing along the front wall of the building, and it made her smile. Within a few minutes, Gilbert had filled the tank, checked the oil, and washed her windshields. He came into the office and offered her a chair.

"So, what's on your mind?"

"Are you Gilbert Porter?" she asked.

"Yes, I am," he responded.

"It is very nice to meet you. My name is Lillian Rooney. Your son, Michael, helped me with a serious problem last year right before he left town, and I need to speak with him. I don't know where he moved to, but could you give me his address and phone number?"

Gilbert sat down at his desk.

"Let me get this straight. You want me to tell you where Michael David Porter, my son, has moved and what's his phone number?"

"Yes, do you know where he is?"

"I do, but are you sure it's my son, Michael, you're looking for?"

"Why, yes. He told me you owned this gas station."

Gilbert sat back in his chair and seemed momentarily speechless. He noticed the gold cross hanging from her necklace.

"Where did you get that necklace, young lady?"

"Do you recognize it, Mr. Porter?"

Gilbert reached out and turned the cross over to see the inscription the jeweler engraved on the back of the cross. It read: To my wonderful son, from Mom, 1957.

"Yes, I do. My wife, Clissie, gave it to him about fifteen years ago. How did you get it?"

"Michael gave it to me."

"I want you to tell me your story. But first, I want to put a sign out by the street that says we're closed so we won't be interrupted."

Within a few minutes, he returned and pulled a shade down, covering the large front window of the office. "Okay, tell me everything and don't leave out any detail. Years from now, you may not remember them, so tell them all to me now. You want a Coca-Cola?"

"Sure!"

Rooney was beginning to feel a chill up her spine. After Gilbert brought in the drinks, he unplugged the phone and said, "I'm ready. I want to hear everything!"

For the next hour, Rooney described every event of her ordeal and rescue. She gave a description of every emotion she had and, more importantly, her interaction with Michael. She began by describing where she had first met Michael at Ben's bar downtown and how she enjoyed listening to Michael play that old piano. After she failed to name a song that he couldn't play, she agreed to meet him at the shelter where he worked. She described the shelter and his work there and then told Gilbert about the lunch date at Washington Park. Finally, she outlined the events of her capture, the three awful days in the barn, and her miraculous rescue. She tearfully described her last meeting with Michael when he said he had another job to do for his boss. He left two days after they found her and the judge. Lastly, she described Michael both physically and emotionally.

Gilbert was speechless for a while as tears formed in his eyes.

"Did I say something wrong?" she asked.

Gilbert wiped the tears from his face. "No, Lillian, you said everything just fine."

"What's wrong? Why are you crying?"

Gilbert took a few moments to regain his composure and said, "You don't know it yet, but you have given me the greatest gift a father could ever receive. I only wish Michael's mother could hear your story, but I know she is aware of it. She died two years ago from cancer, and it has been very lonely around my place ever since. Rooney, would you take a little trip with me? It's just two miles from here, and I want to show you something."

"Sure, I guess so."

Lillian was confused. Why didn't Gilbert just give her Michael's phone number and address and let her go on her way. But she had nothing else to do, so she went along. Gilbert and Lillian left in his VW station wagon and headed south on Grant Street. Within ten minutes, Gilbert turned into Maple Park Cemetery and found his way down the narrow road between the thousands of headstones and monuments.

"Here we are, Lillian. This will take just a few minutes."

Lillian was a little frightened as she got out of the car. She had just met Gilbert Porter, and he wanted to take her to a cemetery. This was really weird, but she followed him as he walked between the headstones and the giant maple, oak, and elm trees that filled the cemetery.

Gilbert stopped at a large headstone and asked Rooney to come around to see the engraving.

"This is what I wanted you to see," he said as he pointed to the beautiful marble headstone that was decorated with fresh flowers on both sides of its base.

Lillian reluctantly walked around to see the headstone engraving that read:

Michael David Porter
Our loving son
Born November 21, 1945
Died December 26, 1959

"You see, Lillian, Michael drowned in a frozen lake at Christmas back in 1959. He was trying to save his dog, Pat, who had fallen through the ice during a hockey game Michael and his brother were having with their friends. He was buried wearing that gold cross you have around your neck. I now know for sure where he is and what God has asked him to do for you and probably countless others. I miss him so much.

"He was born the day before Thanksgiving in 1945, and you bring me this news about what Michael is still doing for others the day before Thanksgiving twenty-six years later on his birthday. I don't think this is just coincidence. I now have the assurance that I will see my son again someday."

Rooney was speechless. Gilbert hugged her neck as the tears began to flow once again like they had done so many times in the past while Gilbert sat there next to Michael's grave. They both sat down and cried. They cried until the tears wouldn't come anymore. Even though they didn't quite understand how it happened, they knew what had happened, and to them it was, indeed, a miracle. It was as Michael had said, "A gift from God."

They returned to the station and chatted awhile before Rooney left for home. Gilbert said he would call her and invite her out to the house very soon—maybe at Christmas time because that holiday had a special meaning to the Porters. There were many mementos of Michael that she might like to see. She was happy to accept.

As she was leaving the station, Rooney said, "I want you to know he now has his own dog, Blue! One more thing, did Michael ever play the piano?"

Gilbert laughed. "He tried to play the piano, but he wasn't any good. Matter of fact, he was awful, and it frustrated him so. He loved to play the piano, but to listen to him practice was very painful for the whole family and probably the neighbors as well."

"Not anymore. He is a master at the piano!"

The emotion overwhelmed Gilbert as he kissed Rooney on the cheek and went back into his office past the old Coca-Cola machine. He sat there for an hour or so just thinking about what had just happened. Rooney headed to Gentle Ben's. After this evening, PJ would likely have to drive her home.

Epilogue

It has been ten years since the life-changing events of September 1970. Lillian Rooney is now Mrs. William Davenport and the mother of twin boys named Michael and David, five years old. They have a photo of young Michael David Porter on their mantle above the fireplace. Their home is on a small farm south of town. It has a lake that Wild Bill has stocked with bass and catfish. Davenport will retire soon from the police force and plans to establish Wild Bill's Detective Agency. He is still looking for the council and vows he will never give up until he finds it. Rooney's practice is still growing, but she plans to retire in a few years and set up a nonprofit organization to help homeless and abused adults and children. She now has a dog, a dachshund named Gus. The family adopted him from the Humane Society, where she volunteers one Saturday each month. Rooney donated a plaque in Michael's honor that was placed in the waiting room at the shelter. It reads:

In Loving Memory
of
Michael David Porter
Friend of the Humane Society

Mr. Porter never fails to invite Rooney and her family to his home during the Christmas holidays. He enjoys playing with the boys, and he plans to take them to their first Major League baseball game in St. Louis one of these days. Gilbert was named their godfather.

Michael's brother, Stephen Lowell Porter, is an associate professor of philosophy and religion at Drury College. He was also named a godfather for Rooney's boys. Stephen is quite a fisherman and enjoys fishing Table Rock Lake with Bill. He has a dog, a Labrador named Max. Stephen is engaged to Pamela, a lovely lady from Gainesville, Missouri.

Vern Hoover is still on Davenport's team. He became so accustomed to Springfield he decided the city was a nice place to raise his kids. Davenport got him to quit smoking, put him on an exercise program with Chip at the fitness center, and taught him how to fish. He didn't get him off chocolate. Bill told him that fish come from a lake, not from the Fifty-First Street Deli in New York City. He likes fishing, but mostly he just likes hanging out with Wild Bill on the lake. The last time they were fishing, Davenport was pulling in a large bass while Vern was eating a bag of Oreo cookies. He looked at Davenport and said, "You know, if they don't have chocolate in Heaven, I may not go!"

Patti Jo and her husband, Russell, live on Lake Springfield south of town. She is a very busy real estate attorney who still joins Rooney at Gentle Ben's several times a week. PJ is now the first chair violinist with the Springfield Symphony. Last year, her husband's basketball team at Drury won the NAIA National Basketball Championship in Kansas City, Missouri. They have two children, a four-year-old daughter named Kate and a two-year-old son named Ben.

The suspects they apprehended refused to cooperate with the prosecutor. No one admitted to the killing of Mr. Albert Richardson, and they refused to provide any information about the council or the kidnapping of the judge and Rooney. They were all found guilty of second-degree murder and kidnapping, for which they received life sentences. They will die in prison.

The Federal Reserve chairman investigated the Southwestern Bank of Springfield and all of its branches to see if any funds were laundered and given to any subversive organizations. They found no evidence that this occurred, and the bank was released from the investigation after two years and with a new president. The new bank president endowed the Springfield Humane Society with considerable funds and helped to establish a nonprofit organization to ensure the facility would always survive and continue to provide the services that Michael had established in his brief time with the shelter. The FBI investigated the Harding family and the Harding Motor Transit Company but found no one else they suspected as being involved with the council or any other organization to which they would funnel money. However, it will be a long time before they are finally dropped from surveillance.

The Honorable Hal Sandrotas pleaded guilty to accepting a bribe that led to the death of Mr. Albert Richardson. He was given a sentence of twenty-five years in a minimum-security federal prison in Forrest City, Arkansas. His law license was permanently revoked. Mrs. Sandrotas divorced Hal, and his children seldom write and never visit him. Hal will be seventy-seven years old when he is released. Thomas Sandrotas was allowed to keep his store, but he makes his loan payments to the United States Department of Justice. No one knows the whereabouts of Lolita.

Ben has now opened his restaurant for lunch and has taken on a partner to help handle his robust business near Park Central Square on South Street. He hired a buddy of his from the Marine Corps who was having trouble finding work after the war. They expanded into a vacant site next door, from which they now offer take-out service, something Ben said he would never do. It was a profitable decision. Gentle Ben's is still the place to be and the place to be seen in downtown Springfield. It's known all over Southwest Missouri as having the best BBQ chicken wings and the friendliest atmosphere you can find anywhere. The piano is still there, but Ben permanently closed the cover to the piano keys. It just didn't seem right to have someone play the piano after Michael.

There has been one other addition to the bar. In the center of the large mirror behind the bar for everyone to see is a large, gold-framed photograph of Michael David Porter, age fourteen, from Springfield, Missouri.

Acknowledgments

I wish to thank Amanda Parsons and her staff for their assistance in publishing my first literary work. It was very important to have Inspiring Voices and Guideposts be a part of this project. I want to thank Pastor Jess Gibson and his staff of the Cornerstone Church and The Manor at Elfindale, who gave me permission to use the image of Elfindale Lake in my book. Their support and encouragement allowed me to tell my story about the magnificent playground the estate has been to many young boys over the years. The work would not have been complete without the contribution of Laura Rhoades-Yokoi of Las Vegas, Nevada, for providing her image of the merry-go-round on the front cover, like the one in Washington Park many years ago. Linda Winders and Johnna Quick of Springfield, Missouri, provided their photograph of Maple Park Cemetery, which was most appreciated, and with which a vital part of the story was told. I want to thank all the family and friends of Springfield, Missouri, who, unknowingly, contributed to this story, and for making my hometown a great place in which to grow up. I want to express my deep appreciation for my wife, Glenda, whose assistance and unwavering love and support, made this project so enjoyable. Lastly, this story was written in memory of those close friends and family members who died much too soon but made my life richer for knowing and loving them.

CPSIA information can be obtained at www.ICGtesting.com
Printed in the USA
BVOW022341300812

299270BV00003B/65/P